Nerissa

BY ELISABETH ROHM

Copyright © 2009 by Elisabeth Rohm

Cover and book design by Lance Barton

All Rights Reserved.

No part of this book may be reproduced in any form or by any electronic or mechanical means including information storage and retrieval systems, without permission in writing from the author. The only exception is by a reviewer, who may quote short excerpts in a review.

Elisabeth Rohm
Visit my website at www.elisabeth-rohm.com

Printed in the United States of America

First Printing: July 2009

NERISSA

Notes from Augusta Weiess

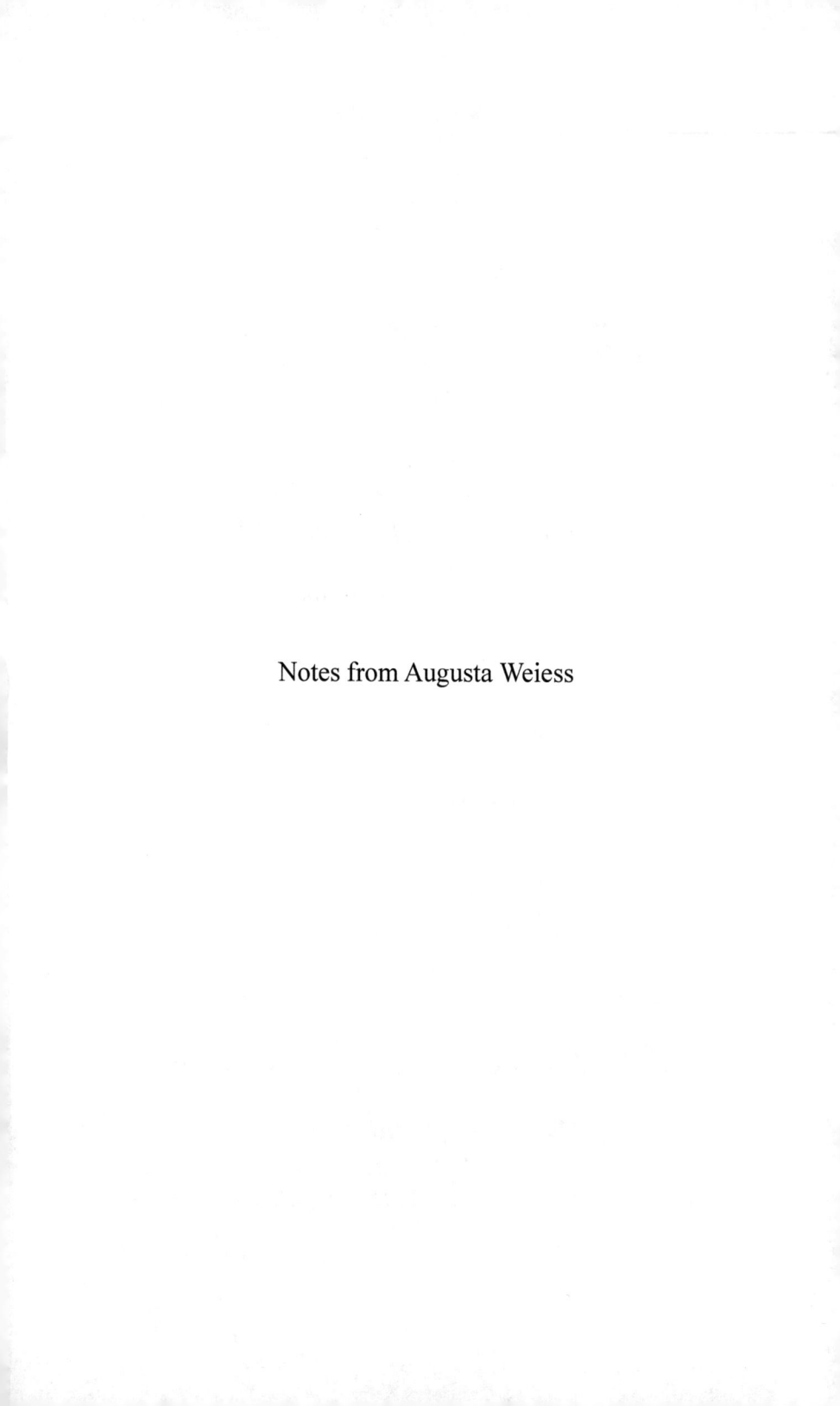

From the cragged coast of Scotland

Gazes down an ancient gray castle.

Where the wild breakers dash high.

There, beside the vaulted window,

Stands a fair woman, sweet and frail,

Pale from suff'ring from bitter ills;

And as she plays her harp she sings,

And the wind is tossing her flowing tresses

And she bears her mournful song

Over the heaving, boundless sea.

I assure you I knew not that I would come across such a woman beforehand. I introduce these words from my childhood to illustrate the predetermined choice of my findings. These words that my father would playfully march through my nightly rituals planted the seed for me to discover her alone in that castle where she had been forgotten and left to blend with history. When I was a child my father used to recite this poem to me. Now it seems as if he was subtly urging me. Maybe it was my father that was meant to find her but that is what we children are left with when our parents die ... all that they have left undone. He would speak to me at night in German. It was something private we shared; a secret character he pulled out with bedtime stories when other people wouldn't think of him as an immigrant. As I would drift off to my dreams most nights those words would traipse through my subconscious like a prayer seeking her.

    When my father passed away all that I had left of him were the pieces of things he planned to do when he retired. Though life for my father never got beyond the possibilities of our small town he had made something of himself even if he hadn't seen the world as he had hoped. Sometimes just showing up and staying where you are is an accomplishment. But I have found that he was not full of longing for another time or place, instead he was drawing me close to something divine in my own life.

This is my journal of those events.

On the third morning of my trip I woke to a bitter cold Thursday wrapped in the starchy sheets of my Inverness lodging. My plan was to drive along the North Sea coast up to the most Northern tip of the Highlands to a place called Duncansby Head. I had once seen poignant photographs of pirouetting cliffs that had been carved out by the Sea and were like skyscrapers dispersed casually amongst the tides, growing from beneath the water. From there I would drive without purpose and end up on the West Coast. Rumor had it that the Isle of Skye could utter things never heard before.

My semi-itinerary, after Duncansby Head, was to stay at any town near it or head Northwest toward Cape Wrath and Durness.

As I was driving along the coast through Dornoch and Lybster I had to get out of the car to smell the air. I was in the highlands and couldn't pass it from a distance. The deeper the imprint, the greater the chance that the same passion would also be passed on to my kids. Can you see this land with huge sky, green as spring should be, with the topography of human curves and purple mists and gray watery skies? Yellow flowers pepper the hills and grow from the rocks like bright splashes from a child's painting. There are a million corners to get found in and valleys where the earth is as rich as birth. I walked for what felt like miles and in that wandering found myself at the start of a long gravel road. As curiosity does it made me turn right. Following its narrow and steep lines the wind became so aggressive that I almost turned back but just in the nick of time saw an elegant iron-gate connected to stone pillars that was opened and as I walked along the circular driveway on scratching yellow pebbles I took in scattered sections of snow and frost that were resting silently on the grounds before a castle. From the flags by the front doors and the excess and inconsistency of car brands and bicycles, it seemed apparent that there was an open house. My Dad was there with me and I could feel his thick, muscular arm go around my shoulder as I walked towards the door.

In that millisecond I became everything I was before things happened to me. My days then were made up of yearning for discoveries. Riding horses and reinventions of my self in sweaty, breathless expeditions in the woods filled my hours. I struck out as I was doing there in

Scotland and wandered down those streets that were foreign, driven by my desire to see what was at the end. I remember once discovering a house a few streets away that was on fire, burning like an inferno. That was the first time color introduced itself to me and it was then that I started to paint. A short fifteen-minute walk and you would find it there still standing but quite charred nonetheless. It was a ninety year old white colonial with black shutters like ours and like most houses in New England. I remember the piano that was in the center of the empty room with its burned keys. Oddly the sheet music had survived and was scattered over the wooden floorboards of the skeleton that was left. The remains projected the frail memories of the family that had lived there and I found it fascinating to meander through the fragments of their world playing broken music that the piano would cough out. I painted for the first time then ... a burned piano ... over and over.

With that same voyeurism I approached the front doors of the castle.

After being received by a caretaker I entered into the main hall. "Aye, welcome miss." He was a frail old man with peppered skin, dappled with shades of discolor. Directing the traffic of the buyers or lookers I was a wanderer and was drawn towards gracious, intricately carved oak doors which when opened, became a ballroom. "Please, enjoy our home." I heard him say behind me. The dust in the air seemed to dance around the arches and pillars hypnotically, so that the ballroom with cobwebs clinging purposefully to the chandelier and stained glass windows looked colorful and not dull or dirty. I was carried away into a memory of times gone by and not at all in the present of that unkempt room. I could feel his soft hand on my side, on my skin, urging me on.

The gray marble floors seemed to heatedly push me into a hallway that led me away from that romantic old ballroom and into a world of tapestries. It was dark and cold but I could see the faded murals of what I thought was a hunt painted on the solid stone floor. I began to feel lost amongst those old heavy tapestries and started to walk somewhat listlessly. I found myself in a room filled with empty pots and planters which seemed to have held trees or flowers at one time. There were wing back chairs and ottomans and the wood floor was draped with red deer skins. This was a room for daydreaming ... a forest inside. Memories breathed around me; the air was heavy with them like the scent of a woman's skin when she has sprayed perfume on after a bath. I sensed the woman of my dreams. Now I try to separate my imagination from reality to see if I knew her face before I saw her eyes and the flat lands of her pale skin.

As I came again into the main hall I saw to my right a view of the water through French glass doors. I slowly wandered there, to my right into that room. It was an impressive library either having belonged to an aristocrat or a writer. Books and books and books lined the dark wood cased walls. The fireplace still had ashes in it and I couldn't help but imagine many nights spent there on the plaid rug and pillows left casually on the floor. I would have lain there for hours on green, red and black plaid; with the night fire and candles to light this dark Scotland ... unlike any place I've ever been. The fabric on the chairs was worn where one can rest their elbows. Everything had been petrified, unchanged but for the dust that had collected. Yet, what struck me most profoundly was the view of the water and as I turned purposefully to the French doors that lead outside I saw a sheet hanging over what I knew to be an easel. I smiled to myself, happy to know painting had happened there. Still, I was drawn to the sea. The Veranda seemed to hang over the cliff and I can't ever recall having been as close to the water and sky at the same time before or after.

An unkempt Labyrinth was growing towards the right at the bottom of those twenty slate steps, near to the edge. Before entering it, along the cliff was an almost hidden narrow stone stairway that lead down to the sand and rocks. But, it was getting dark and I was too scared to walk down it. The mist was thickening into quilted folds around me.

Before I went out through the front doors, two feet thick with wood, I turned back to ask the caretaker the length of the sale. I watched his weathered face as he said, with a stiff jaw, that the owner had died some months ago at the age of ninety-four and had left everything to his daughter who was an American. Was he ninety-four too, I wondered? She would be arriving in a couple of days to close everything completely, he continued.

Walking back to my car, which had to have been almost a mile away, I wandered in and out of the rooms I hadn't seen yet. I decided that I would gather my bags and move to the town of Wick which was the closest village to that castle and also far more convenient to Duncansby Head. I still had to see that Modern art of the Ocean. After gathering my belongings at The Inverness Lodge I drove and finally ended up at a simply rustic bed & breakfast. After fully unpacking I bathed and went downstairs to indulge myself in a decadent dinner of goose, in which I found the wishbone. Exhausted from the many miles of walking I fell asleep to dreams of Scotland. Aye, that I did. Dream upon dream of air laced with the sounds of my cold, sleepy feet walking through wet grass.

Very early the next morning I drove up to Duncansby Head. The air was filled and lifted with a frozen mist that reminded me of night prayers and my day moved slowly like a person's chest when they are sleeping. In that mental fog, I lost myself to miles of walking again but this time along the beach. Far from the skyscrapers where I began in the dawn I saw narrow stone stairs that led straight up the entire cliff. It was still morning and only animals seemed to be awake with me. Breathless from the height I ended up by the veranda and labyrinth as if intentionally. The landscaping was paint worthy with lines and symmetry that were architectural, yet its slopes and hidden spots had the suppleness of a woman's body. When I came full circle I went into the labyrinth. I had never been in one and was curious about the inevitability of getting lost. That I did, amongst the hedges that had abandoned much of their shape and were almost canopied as they connected recklessly. I had not forgotten her in my search and was moved by the familiarity of the place.

In a daze I went inside to find out if I might be able to pay for some food. I needed to eat something before I braved the icy walk back. The same older gentleman said that the closest pub was in the village of Wick but then let out a tender smile and said that if I found my way to the kitchen there would be an old woman that was the cook who might give me a bit of soup and some bread. She was there and she did feed me and I was grateful. When I left that day I felt more complete than I had in too long. I had always felt my father had made sacrifices for me and that I had taken so much. In that moment I was able to finally give something back to him. Knowing that I would be returning to that house I easily left to continue the rest of my trip.

I drove Southwest, over the old bridge and the Kyle. The colors that loomed ahead as I drove to the Isle of Skye (derived from Sgaith ... winged island) recall the texture of cat's eyes in its iridescence. The cool waters that reflect heights all around it mixed with the green and black cliffs were created unlike any other part of Scotland because of the intense volcanic activity during the Tertiary Period and glacial erosion during the Ice Age. It is sleek and rural at the same time and to tell of pubs and Inns is to shortchange the experience of its views. As when I ride and know the hidden life of upstate New York I found otters and birds living amongst the castles and valley; so many animals unique to that island. But it is the legends, the Gaelic legends one hears along the way. One must come for that because legends are the things that give us hope, like fables from childhood where the imagination begins. We must have others journeys to begin with before we can know what we hunger for. People need stories to measure themselves against like the ones my Dad gave to me. When we talk of legends we do not only refer to a myriad of illusions but more importantly to fantasy. I believe all great things come from dreams. Many of my paintings come in the dark of dreaming. Two days on the Isle of Skye has given me a lifetime of material. I also, of course, visited Cape Wrath and the Northwest before Skye, but that is another story.

I woke early that morning days later, hungry to get back to the castle. It was my last full day in Scotland and I knew, as I drank my morning tea and ate a grainy, full meal that this was to be my last encounter with a place that had seemed studied before I had ever gotten there. To end there made sense. As I scanned the contents of the house, in my mind's eye, for a purchase that would be sure to grant me an invitation, even at her time of grief, I thought of the easel in the Library.

There was a navy Bentley in the drive. The old man I mentioned before answered the door once again and for the last time. I told him that I had forgotten to buy the easel in the library. He walked with me to see if it was still there. It was. As I was paying him for it I heard a female voice call out to him. Excusing him self momentarily, I presumptuously followed, knowing it was my opportunity. She had a box in her hand that she needed help with. Turning around she almost dropped it as she looked at my face. As I fumbled for an apology she carefully uttered my name ... 'August Weiss'. My awkwardness turned to caution as we looked at each other in amazement, both at a loss for words. Striking to look at; sunset red, curly hair pulled back neatly, pale, sparingly freckled skin, sea-green eyes set evenly. I had no sense of who she was although I felt I had seen her before. It was minutes before either of us said a word.

She explained to me that her name was Estelle Lochalsh and that she owned a gallery in SoHo. She and my agent had been going over my work and discussing an exhibit. I had know about this and been awaiting the decision that was to come post holiday. It would be an enormous break for me. To show at LOCHALSH basically makes your paintings known worldwide and I had been anxious about her seal of approval. The gallery specialized in women's art and I so wanted to hang there amongst her chosen. She was a Guru in my world.

Estelle asked why I was in Scotland and if I had plans for lunch. I mused on that question. Why was I there?

I was honored to talk to her about art and was excited by her, but chose to stick with what I knew well. I spoke of my Father with trepidation because I wanted her to know that I knew the story of Fathers and Daughters and of the ultimate loss. A Father can stir responses in you that you never knew existed. A Father could make you do almost anything. I knew. I knew.

Eventually we spoke of my work. As I told her of my most recent project (a pair of paintings) I realized in describing them for the first time that they resembled the cliffs and the water there. They were a new chapter for me as an artist. I had often chalked landscapes in my journals but never painted them as my subject; usually just faces and bodies. The physicality of people moved me. But one night before my trip I woke to paint, as I often do. I remembered that the heat wasn't working that New York winter night and I had to bundle up so much that the sleeve of my sweater kept grazing my pallet. During my last week I worked on that pair of paintings. They are very similar images but one was a masculine interpretation and the other was a feminine version. I categorized them by gender only because in both there was a figure wandering the cliffs, one was male and the other was female.

I had always heard that Estelle was cold but I found her to be full of power and earned humor. At the time I thought with certainty that I'd found the sad girl in the castle and couldn't believe the serendipity of my father's urgings so long ago.

Estelle was inspired to tell me of her grandmother Nerissa Lochalsh. As it turned out her grandmother painted in France in the early to mid-nineteen hundreds, but under a masculine name. Actually, I knew his work rather well and was particularly fond of it. It was unsettling to realize I had always revered him. Yes, there were female artists at the time, which were known as women, but they struggled with countless prejudices. Reminded again about the history of my own gender I was flooded with gratitude for having to primarily focus on the success of my work as a painter, not my paintings as a woman. It made sense to me now why Estelle had the bias she did.

She spent a couple of hours showing me Nerissa's paintings, which were scattered, amongst the many bedrooms on the private floors. Estelle explained to me that the Impressionists had heavily influenced Nerissa's painting because Cassat and Degas had been family friends. Yet, she had simplicity and a sense of longing in her work that made them modern. In her portrayals there is a meeting in flesh. I got the smell at the back of my throat as I glanced at women's faces that transfixed me with the close gaze of their watery eyes. Her work awakened every breath that had ever passed through its halls and I was there, suddenly, in the past with her on those hours when her work became whole and was hung. Estelle shared with me her idea of exhibiting Nerissa's work in New York, which I fully reciprocated enthusiasm about. It had always occurred to me that doing an exhibit of "unknowns" who had been famous under another identity would be a great piece of controversy.

    She told me all about her family's history as she took me on this tour. Somehow, lunch turned into hours and then dinner. I understood the exchange well because I too had lost a parent then and sometimes it was easiest to spend time with a stranger. She invited me to stay the night. I slept in the sweetest little girl's room that was drizzled with Highland greens and yellows. I slept well. In the morning we had breakfast and discussed fate. We then made plans to meet in New York the following week.

On my way back to the village I recalled pictures from the history she had shared. I thought of it all with amazement, bewildered by the events life ceaselessly brings and knew to the core, as we do sometimes, that everything does happen for a reason. When I got back to Wick I began to pack for New York. I had one afternoon left and decided to go up to the Highlands to paint. I purposefully had left my supplies at home so that I would take a break in Scotland, but I had the must, the urge that it takes to do good work. I went to a local arts and crafts store and bought paint. With Nerissa's easel and her basically spotless canvas I drove smack into the mid-west Highlands where I found myself in hills of green and yellow and white. I sat on a rock. With paint in my veins I sat to paint what I saw: green, yellow and white. I painted for about an hour when other seasons showed up and I needed a different brush. Searching desperately for my tool I scoured the drawer of her easel. In the back was a small leather folder filled with yellowed papers. I took off the string that was tied around it and flipped through the pages when I noticed paintings, inks and sketches. They drew me in and I forgot all about the brush and my work. It was her diary. Nerissa whispered me into her life. Nothing moved for hours except fingertips. I wasn't there anymore. My shutter-speed movements were like the twitching of sleep as I lived with her that fall in 1911. This was the girl I had dreamed of that lived in the castle. Nerissa, the painter, was who I had come to find.

Only as the light began to shift was I brought back to the present and the fact that I had to go to the airport. So, with easel in hand I ran back to the car and drove madly to the Inn. I grabbed my carry-on bag and loaded myself into the taxi. Getting to the Edinburgh Airport in the nick of time, I settled in and continued in her words. In London I burned through the tediousness of travel, cleaned up at the Hotel in Chelsea and walked to an old tavern I used to love reading at. The Black Harp had four fireplaces and big cozy chairs where I was able to read her words over and over, so as to never finish.

In New York I prepared for my meeting with Estelle. The exhibit had been green-lit and she needed to go through my collection. I hadn't yet called to tell her of the journal. It wasn't that I wanted to keep them instead it was that I had read them without her knowing and felt awkward about it. Nevertheless, I couldn't wait to see her. With portfolio in hand and the journal in a small Kiehl's shopping bag I arrived for the long afternoon ahead.

First things first: "... I found a journal from 1911 that I believe was your grandmother's. I have it here for you," I fumbled to get it in my hands to pass to her, "I read it." What would her response be?

"Oh, my God, that's fabulous. Don't tell me a thing. I can't wait to read this." She said as she turned the yellow pages over and over delicately.

After hours of work our heads ached from the strain of our eyes. We packed it in and wandered down to Rauel's to have a glass of red wine. It was winter still. Nestling in the clock ticked forward and became dinner. Two minds are greater than one and I adhere to the rule that intellectual dialogue is worth the time it takes. Finally separating I went home buoyant from my new relationship. Bleary from exhaustion I fell asleep only to be awakened by my phone ringing at ten am. Estelle had spent the morning reading the journal entries. She wanted to talk.

After purging ourselves we then discussed the idea of publishing them. For the past nine months we have been putting this together. So my "prologue" is an explanation of what? How Nerissa came to be a part of my life, as she will become a part of yours? That is a given. As a friend once said, "The barn has burned down ... now I can see the moon." I was meant to find these journal entries, just as my Dad was meant to point me towards them. Through my journey I have let go of the physical plain and locked eyes with the unknown. There she was as I'd imagined faded and alone within the walls of a castle maybe to be forgotten but waiting to be discovered like myself and possibly like you, Dear Reader.

At some point in Scotland my father left (I could feel him lift off) satiated I'm sure by our discoveries. In most cases people don't miss what they don't know but, I believe he had longed for much more because, he was knowledgeable. Instead he had taken care of me which had limited him. He was a man that stayed at home but I don't think he regretted that decision in the end.

Nerissa Jacqueline Wemyss Lochalsh

Diary

August - October 1911

17 August, 1911

No one is saying the word. Suicide. Why can't we say it when it's the truth? There was no accident. Even I am a liar as I wait, like a beggar, on a bit of mercy, some reconciliation, some erasing of the moment. "Please come take the truth away and bury it not him!" Marlowe used to tell me that I should write my way out of the overwhelming moments; vanish in expression. Since I can't seem to get up off my pleading knees maybe writing will help me like it always seemed to help him.

I shall try to begin here ... today I had to bury my husband. Last night I couldn't sleep in our bed and yet I couldn't leave our bedroom. I sat paralyzed on the floor by his desk and drank the last half of the whiskey hoping that it would take me to him. I needed us to be close so we spoke through the night and shared the antics of drunken discussion. I know Crispen must have been concerned for me but he let me be until it was time to come to this place that has taken my purpose and buried him in earth. Though no one spoke to me last night nor today my head is filled with noise like a cymbal being played and I quite appreciate Crispen's silence.

I cannot remember what time it was when Crispen sent Odette up to dress me. Yet, I do remember that I sent her out crying. I feel sorry for that, but Marlowe and I were discussing the people that would be at the funeral and I didn't want to be bothered. I told Crispen that he could come in and pick out my dress but that I may not be going ... I had a stomachache. He looked at me openly as he does, not pretending that I was behaving properly but recognizing that I might never be again the way I was. How does one heal when half of their soul and body no longer exists?

Quite simply he has been a part of my life since the day I was born and I do not know ... but I cannot think about that right now ... I'm trying to write my way out of this cemetery. I cannot leave though. To leave without his hand in mine is too finite and I would rather sit here. Close. How can I digest that he is gone when he is still in my blood, in the most tangible, fleshiest part of myself and is very much alive around me. To walk away from his grave is strangling and I am tight from the choking of death myself. I truly can't bear the pain. I may have to sleep here.

This morning is a nauseating blur. In fact, I feel numb from the whiskey and lack of sleep. However, I do remember Crispen sending Mama up to help me bathe and dress, after I had terrified Odette. This made me even more hysterical. I am sure I disturbed the household but I do not care. I am not ashamed. They should leave me be. I can't remember how I got dressed actually. My memory of last night was our talk, our endlessness. His sweet words drinking into my blood. Last night we made our usual love with only words. Then I still made sense in my world within these walls. Yet, when they interrupted, when they forced their words of pity on me by attempting to wash my face and make me presentable it left, sense left.

At the cemetery I stopped being the woman I am, the light in me crept away and I disappeared into the hateful person I am in this moment, this echoing moment. I was disgusted with this place and despised everyone for being here. I had contempt for all of them because they stood there, around his grave, reminding me that this is very real and that he is not coming back.

During the ceremony I stood as far away as possible, leaning against a small tree. Humming it away, I was consumed by the low, funeral gray sky, and the dampness that's still sticking to my skin. It has not rained today but it will. One can tell in Scotland because of the dark brown smell that clings to the fibers of air. That is how I will remember today! I will recall the disease of my life with the smell of the coming rain and the earth of the grave choking me. And yes, of course, my dear, dear friends and family all catching glances of me. How dare they indulge themselves in my broken heart. I could tell by how many times they were looking at me during the burial that I was humming rather loudly, but I was trying to remember the words to a song we sang as children. I don't see what is so wrong with that. I was not going to stand there sobbing about him being gone.

At the end of that dirty earth ritual, that performance of tears and stale traditions I became trapped by my tree as everyone slowly, sleepwalked past me mumbling. I'm sure they worry that I've developed that condition where one loses the ability to communicate due to trauma, but I've made a conscious decision to not talk to their bulging, swollen faces. Somewhere in the middle of someone's pointless words of pity I turned away and finally walked to your grave. They have no concept of our life nor do they conceive of the loss, they are absolutely mistaken in their ability to console.

God help me, all I want to do is be buried in there with you. My body feels hollow, like my muscles have evaporated and I am crumbled here now. Looking in, looking up. Why no mercy for me? I know, in the echo of no relief, that I will never see your beautiful face again. I see the freshly piled earth and all the flowers ... I see it and smell it and I curse you God for now it is real. These words cannot help. I will not come back here.

But, I can't leave you here Marlowe, I can't leave you in this cemetery that smells like rain and death. I can't leave your side because you are my way home and without you I will be a wanderer. Oh sweet, how is this our destiny?

I can't write anymore in this ridiculous diary! The sound of my voice in my head mocks me. I can't express myself like you could. I'm only doing this because you used to tell me that you wrote to write your way out of yourself. When you were consumed by something, trapped by it in your mind you would write yourself back into your life. That's why I am sitting here in this cemetery writing. I am trapped inside my memory of you. I can't speak, or think ... I can't even cry anymore. My body fails me. I'm left here with you and yet knowing you're not here and that I'm beginning to lose my mind. They are waiting for me; hoping I will pull myself off the grave and start behaving like a lady again. "Get up Nerissa you child! Get up and walk to the carriage!"

The sky is wavering between light and dark like the way dreams appear. I wish they would leave me here. They wear pity well but have no compassion. They don't know what it's like to have your map taken away when you are in the middle of your journey. He was my way and without him I don't believe that I am whole nor have a purpose. I know that is pitiful, but it is the truth.

I can't write anymore.

I am going to walk to our carriage now and go to the castle ... I want to sleep.

18 August, 1911

Dear Diary, Mama just left me in a fury on the account that I would not speak to her. I lay in bed looking out the window. It was a beautifully quiet sunrise and I couldn't bear to engage in her sort of chatter. Besides, she had been sent by Papa to find me. "Where, oh where have you been since the funeral, my darling!" I wanted to scream at the top of my lungs "DO NOT SAY THAT WORD IN MY PRESENCE!" I am so relieved to have her gone and to be alone. Her presence makes my stomach nauseous and my head throb. I need my solitude ... always have. I feel peaceful lying here and watching the sun quietly creep in through the lace curtains behind my bed. I must have fallen asleep out on the rocks ... Crispen probably carried me inside. He watches me.

Predictably, Papa thinks that I have become hysterical. I imagine his way of handling this will be to not speak to me. He hasn't spoken to me since the morning Odette found Marlowe, nothing at the burial. Oh, he never understood me. He is the last person on the face of the earth that I would speak to about this experience. He doesn't know how to do things purely out of love. He didn't marry my mother out of love. He married her because it was the proper thing to do: she was a good match. I'm sure he is wandering about the castle this morning so I should probably stay in here to avoid his judgments. He has always thought that I walk that very fine line between, as they say it, sanity and insanity. "Well, I suppose I am finally proving you right Papa! I'm not well and probably never will be. So you can go tell Mama you are right once again. You can tell her that your fragile little girl has finally cracked and that it is time for all of you to go back to Paris. Tell her that nothing can be done for me now, that there is no return from this place. Where I am living now people don't speak, they yell or sing. They fantasize about how to remove themselves from this world without anyone noticing!" That is me now and I am content here.

I wish they would go back to Paris actually. Would they leave and give me privacy I might have time to think. I was a little girl here with them, but I also was an adult here with my husband. This is our house and I need complete silence amongst our things so that I can say goodbye. I know that I need the staff although I wish they were gone. I hate how they peek at me from around the corners and the thought of seeing someone's face besides Marlowe's makes me ... oh, his face. It was breathtaking. His eyes were so full. He always said we had the same green-gray eyes you could see to the end of. M. said that when God created us for each other, so many years apart, he left us that one clue. When we looked into each other's eyes, it was like looking at our own selves in the mirror. That is what we were for each other. He knew everything I was feeling before I had to tell him. I knew what he longed for before he had to tell me. We filled each other in the ways that we were empty. I gave Marlowe relief from his sorrow with my innocence and he gave me strength through his passion. He helped me to find painting. If only my parents believed that my painting is so much more than a way to pass time and that it is work that I have great potential in. I can't think about them now. I want to close my eyes and see Marlowe's face ... his lips are full and the perfect shade of bitten red. They are always so warm and the way they kissed mine. Complete abandonment ... we would kiss each other with no fear of disappearing. He was my first kiss. I was sixteen and it was the most terrifying and thrilling day of my life. Oh, M.

No, no, no ... back to painting my angel's face. His nose had a slight bump on it, which looked rough. Pale as air. His eyes ... he was right, he wasn't just a romantic. It was the strangest thing but we really did have the exact same color eyes: the sea on a calm morning when you can see to the bottom. He was perfectly Scottish; pitch, light and with penetrating eyes. That is how I got my name actually. Everything came from him.

The day I was born everyone was here! It was during one of our summer holidays. Marlowe had just turned seventeen and was causing a stir for himself in Paris when he received a letter from my Papa saying that my mother was pregnant. Marlowe had always been very close to my father. There was no guidance or criticism he could not accept from Uncle Randal. Also he was finished with the Paris days and desperate to get home as he later told me. He and his father prepared and traveled, reaching Scotland in time for me a couple of nights later!

After my birth Marlowe asked to hold me and being like family I was handed to him. As he tells it, he looked at my eyes and looked at my parents and said "Nerissa." He said, "Look, her eyes are the color of the sea" and being mesmerized by this little baby in his arms he just muttered to himself again, shaking his head in disbelief of the purity in that moment. He looked at my parents and said, "Nerissa means "of the sea" in Latin, you should name her Nerissa because of the color of her eyes." Mama just laughed and said, "Well what if her eyes change color like most infants?" But somehow the name remained, as did the color of my eyes. Of course I do not really remember such things ... I'm not mad enough to think that. But that is how my husband told it to me.

Back to my memory of his exquisite face ... his hair was fine and void black. It was a bit tousled and never completely proper looking. In fact it always looked like he had just gotten out of bed ... like a little boy. Marlowe always loved my hair ... my red hair. He loved the color and the curls. He loved everything about me ... he loved me.

I hate it here in this room ... I don't belong here ... I need to be in our bedroom! It's the proper place for a wife to be, with her husband in their chambers! I'll have to find the back way. I hope that I don't run into any of the servants out there. I can't stand them looking at my tear stained face with pity ... I just can't stand that!

19 August, 1911, our chambers

Smells, how I hate them; they are hot and sticky with memories. In an attempt to hide I have walked straight into a cobweb of memories. And in my desperate need to avoid him and the truth of the moment I have now become overly aware of his absence. I can't live a lie.

Curled on our bed it's as if time has taken one enormous breath and is holding it painfully in it's lungs. I am suffocating. I need him so desperately to be here. I can't be in this room alone now. I can't read my old Diary's; read about the times that don't exist anymore. I refuse to sit here pretending. I am not ill. I know he's gone.

I want to open the windows. It is too dark now for morning. How I love dawn. The water is praying and the cliffs, which can be violent in height, are magnificent in their grandeur. I love Scotland more than any other country. Marlowe used to ... I can't say that; "used to, used to." Marlowe has a love for the morning also! Oh, I can't do this ... I can't do this!

I don't know where to go, which way to move ... to sit here pathetically or jump out of this window. Oh dearest Diary, I wish for silence, for my heart to be a box I could close the lid on.

M., how could you leave me? How could you drown yourself ... How did I fail you? Do you hear me out there? I am all alone Marlowe! I hate my family, I have no friends, you are my life and you've left me alone! Can't you give me a sign of what to do ... can't you just come back for one night? I just need you to hold me again for one night.

I am losing grasp of my threads. I am afraid to move, tears roll down my face so that I can barely see, yet no sound comes out of me. I didn't plan for this. I didn't expect this. Dear, dear God the light is hurting my eyes. I wish someone would come in here, close the curtains, bring me some water, wipe my hair from my face and end this! I can't breathe well.

Why was it so easy for him to end it and impossible for me to? More than anything I want to die, yet the more I want it the more collapsed I become. Oh, just stop Nerissa, just stop for one minute and pretend Marlowe is here. What would he say to you, how would he guide you?

If Marlowe were here he would wipe my hair from my face and the tears with his fingertips. He would hold me tightly in his arms and then walk me over to the windows with his back facing them so I could look out. He would ask me what I see "What is out there my angel? Look out at the water, smell it, see the sky, look out at the water and remember how beautiful the world is ... remember that it is up to us if we find pleasure or pain in it." Marlowe then would walk me to the washbasin and clean my face. We would walk back into the bedroom, he would close the curtains and all of a sudden the feelings from before would become gentle. Like the sunlight being taken from the room my fears and pain would quiet and ease away. He would then tell me to sleep ... because everything is better after rest. Rocking me, he would somehow trace the outline of my soul and as my eyes would finally close I would barely see the corners of the room or the shape of my feelings. He pacified me and sleep would come. As I lie in this too-empty bed, my pain feels medicated with his memory.

    I am rocking, rocking myself to sleep. I hope I never wake up. I wish, God, I truly wish as I catch my last glance at these walls that are suffocating me that you would be merciful. Grant me a way out here ... don't let me wake up in this room alone with his smell terrorizing me.

20 August, 1911

Dear Diary, I woke up from the sound of my own sobbing and nausea that was curdling inside of me; I had dreamt that Marlowe died. When I became more awake I felt Marlowe's warm hand touching mine and as I turned over to curl into his arms to tell him about my horrid nightmare ... "M., I had a terrible dream that you died and that I was left" ... But he wasn't there. Closing my eyes I counted to ten. He wasn't there.

I didn't know what day or time it was ... I lay there trying to figure it out by sunrises and sunsets. I did recall seeing more than one sunrise and sunset in the past ... I was so certain that I hadn't seen anyone but Marlowe. I was becoming confused by the shadows surrounding me. The castle was too still; that deep silence that is alive. The wind that creeps in at night sounds like whispers and as I pulled on my white dressing gown to see who was there I wiped the tears from my face with the back of my hand and stumbled to the door. I felt numb. There was nothing except darkness. I moved to the windows to see if Marlowe was by the sea. When I opened the curtains they started to whip out at my face from the heavy winds. Still half asleep, I kept pushing them aside with my body clumsily and began to call out his name like I've always done when I needed him at night. There was no answer. I lifted myself up onto the windows edge so that I could look out at the stairs ... "Marlowe?" All I could hear was the empty echo of my voice and the wind that carried it away. When I turned back into the room everything was pitch because of the moonlight hitting my eyes and I became scattered. I was convinced that something might have happened to Marlowe out by the water. That he had drunk too much and had maybe fallen asleep. The shadows began to taunt me ... they chased me out of our room down the stairs. I had to find ... I needed him to hold me ... he always holds me when I have nightmares.

When I got down to the main corridor I began to run with complete direction because I was violently realizing that I had not dreamt that Marlowe had died. What I had dreamt was that Marlowe was here. My nightmare had been that he had come back ... somehow I thought if I slept enough I could sleep him back into my life. I foolishly thought I could dream him back into life!

What I wanted then suited the night perfectly! Scotland has these evenings where the wind convulses and the water is at the mercy of nothing. Night's that rush with a strength that can devour the frailty of flesh and bone. These are the night's you would not wish to be aboard a ship. These are the nights you drop anchor at a port on the North Sea and leave sailing for the daylight hours. I wanted to die in that tumultuous sea. I truly desired to drown and I knew that on a night such as this one I most certainly would. I knew it clearly as I ran towards this thought: I would be with my husband. Nothing left an impression on me except for the cold marble stairs, which were biting and only pushing me further. I promised myself, over and over, as I tore down the halls that I would dive deep into our smashing pitch sea until I found him and he would hold me in his wet heavy arms. He would hold me. I was clear. Defined again.

At the last few steps I stopped. Everything became a blur; I didn't know if Marlowe was gone or writing by the sea, I didn't know if I was awake or dreaming. My reality was injected with an opium. I grasped the iron railing as hard as I could in hopes that the pain of it digging into my skin would wake me. The front of my dressing gown was sticking to my skin cold and void of comfort. Hypnotized by my need to be with M. I continued down, through the hall, into the library, and to the door. In that moment I wanted to drown so desperately I could taste the salt. Call it a conscience. Call it God's will.

I flew back up those stairs. The shadows from the deer's antlers on the walls seemed to come alive around me, ghosts that were trying to stop me from the delusion. I must have been sobbing unabashedly because as I got to the second level of stairs someone touched my shoulder. As I whipped around, I saw Odette there in her dressing gown holding a night candle. We stood there startled, like figments of the others imagination. I had no energy left. I collapsed to the floor. There were no more tears ... there was nothing.

Poor Odette must have thought her mistress had lost her mind. "Miss, I think you might like to have a bit of soup. You haven't eaten any supper in three days. I'll wake Crispen to get you to the library for a bit of soup." Maybe I screamed at her ... I really cannot remember. Maybe I did nothing but lay there motionless. What may have been brief moments seemed an eternity, but finally arms gathered me close. I opened my eyes and looked into Crispen's. All I could think to say was "Don't bring me out to the sea ... don't bring me out to the sea ... I can't bare not seeing him there."

Crispen brought me into the servant's kitchen and told me that I needed to eat. I said I couldn't bear to eat anything! For the first time in many years he spoke gruffly. He said "Aye, Miss Nerissa you are going to eat a wee bit of supper!" So, I ate. I was more ravenous than ever. I devoured fresh baked grain bread, hot vegetable stew, and Crispen's incessant humming of a lullaby. It's strange but I do believe that was the song that I tried to hum at Marlowe's funeral. Crispen must have taught it to us when we were children ...

> "O, Thou, who kindly dost provide
>
> For every creature's want!
>
> We bless thee, God of nature wide,
>
> For all thy goodness lent:
>
> And, if it please these heavenly guide,
>
> May never worse be sent;
>
> But whether granted or denied,
>
> Lord bless us with content!"

Crispen carried me to my childhood bedroom. As I lie here writing about why I didn't do it I find myself staring at this room in wonderment. Though I know it is healing for me to be here I am forced to question how this could have ever been me. I don't have this innocence anymore. I am lost in lace and delicate porcelain toys of girlhood. The colors are so different from the rest of the house. Light ... everything is light in here. The greens and yellows are fragile like the wisps of color at dawn. Oh my, look at all the dolls. I had almost forgotten that I collected dolls. I also collected these china horses ... many beautiful horses from different lands across the sea. This little girl's room that I had forgotten about was who I was before us, before I became his wife and it is a balm for my spirit to wander through these memories. If I close my eyes I can hear my parents voices echo from those years and behind my eyelids I see myself before I married. If I can recall that girl I will be able to begin again. I suppose that's why I am writing here in bed. I figure that if I can clarify for myself who I am, at the core, I won't be afraid to live. I know I'll deserve it. I won't have to be afraid to fall asleep or wake up. I won't have to worry about dreams or sorrow overcoming me and making me do irrational things.

Somehow eating supper tranquilized me. All I hope for now is to sleep like the rest of the castle and to wake in daylight not darkness. I pray dear God that when I wake up I will remember and believe that Marlowe is gone. When I open my eyes again I may still have salt on my face from the tears shed, but I will be reconciled. Marlowe is gone but I'm right here, alive! No more thoughts of death.

Maybe I can spend tomorrow painting. I miss myself ... the me I am when I work. I miss the textured smell of my essence; my flight of color. If Marlowe could write himself back into his life, maybe I can paint myself back into mine ... without him. I know I'll never stop wishing though.

One day when I was in Paris, I must have been eleven years old, I received a letter from him. In it he wrote a fairy tale for me that told of the sea being created by the tears of two lovers who were on separate soil and far from each other. As I lie here remembering his words I see myself kneeling at the edge of that water trying to reconcile myself with the loss of land.

Sweet soul forbid thyself and except thy condition ... sleep in your innocent girlish dreams again and let them absorb the demons in your heart. I now know why God gave me talent: painting is my survival. Now I lay me down to sleep, I pray the lord my soul to keep. If I should die before I wake, I pray the lord my soul to take ... Amen.

Goodnight M.

21 August, 1911

Dearest Diary,

How marvelous to be awakened by the sound of the birds that hover around our sea here. It is quite lovely sleeping in my childhood bedroom again! I feel completely refreshed. I must be better for I have slight pains in my belly from hunger. I should ring for Odette to bathe and dress me. She can retrieve my dressing garments from upstairs. In fact I think I shall have all my personals brought down here. I should think that would be quite suitable.

Also, I will join the family for breakfast. That should get a rise out of them. My father will have to control himself from having an attack of some kind for he will be in such a state of shock from the witnessing of my joy. Mama of course will sit there in her cushioned seat wondering how long it will be before I completely upset everyone. They always watch expectantly. I rather enjoy how nervous I make them all! I find it amusing. "The poor, fragile girl has always has a propensity towards breakdowns." Dr. Mac Lachlan has said to them on more than one occasion but I don't suffer from his labeling me. I've heard many say this, not just him. Of course it is untrue. They are just unaccustomed to a woman being emotional and opinionated. Yet, I do know my reputation.

When I work on the cliffs today I shan't surprise them at all. They will find it eccentric, which is how they see me. They have witnessed me painting many times but do not take it seriously. They deem it entertainment, equal to a womanly pastime. "It isn't ladylike." They do not understand that as an artist you must go to where your subject is either physically or emotionally no matter how uncomfortable. Being an artist takes one far away from rules of any kind. Actually they do understand artists. The truth is, they simply do not view me as one. How dare they, they who have not even studied one of them, who only glance at me from a distance and assume my worth and ability.

I know Papa will avoid me today despite my sudden glorious return to myself. No words of wisdom or tenderness; no moment shared. You see Dear Diary, the more alive and passionate I am the more afraid he is. He can't bear to watch his precious girl behave so outlandishly! I embarrass him. Yet, I have often found that those who worry about others are only avoiding worrying about themselves. I wish he would go back to Paris and work on his "magnificent" cathedral and leave me alone. He is a constant reminder of what I fear in life; prejudice and callousness. I most certainly did not inherit my affectionate nature from him.

But, today I will make beautiful. No tears. No Marlowe. Manners and smiles. I shall wear my skye blue summer dress. I think my pearls should be perfect. Today is going to be wonderful, dripping with skye blue and pearls! Everyone will be joyful ... I will declare it. I will march into the breakfast quarters and announce that the mourning period is over! In fact, maybe we should have our annual summer festivities. Yes, we should have our ball!

I haven't worn this dress since the day M. asked me to marry him ...

On the night before he asked for my hand Marlowe and my father had stayed up much later than the others had. I remember listening to their conversation crouched on a lower stair as if prepared for flight. I must have listened for over an hour and yet I never heard any such question posed. Still, I knew that somewhere in their evening the question had been asked and permission granted.

As I lay in bed that night I envisioned the wedding day from beginning to end. I saw the dressing period and the swirls of white. I heard the laughter as the women gathered to help me dress. I saw the garden become decorated outside my window. I saw Marlowe's outline waiting for me as I walked down the aisle and felt his hand hold mine as the priest's words washed over me. Stained glass glittered through the lace of my veil and when it was lifted from my face I saw his. As I looked into those beloved eyes I had no idea what would happen next but I knew it would be grand. All this I thought and dreamt of as I lay in my bed that anxious night!

Sleeping restlessly I woke exhausted to a hot morning. The rest of the house was off in slumber so I tiptoed down to Odette's room to fetch her. She returned with me and put me in my skye blue dress, pulled my too heavy red hair away from my face and chose the pearls as crescendo, before I excitedly ran down the stairs in anticipation. I could hear the clinging of the silverware as the girls set the table in the dinning room. Surprisingly, Papa was in the music room pensively looking at the sea. I went up to him and embraced him, "What a beautiful morning!" When I pulled away he held me tightly. He held me ... it felt as if many minutes had passed. Then he stepped back and touched my hair and told me of the fine beauty I possessed and how he had always put me on a pedestal. He spoke tenderly and said that if I had ever been sad about his distance, I should know it had always been because I was on that pedestal and it was hard for him to reach that high sometimes. He told me about his many memories of my childhood and of all the wonderful times he had remembered sharing. He looked me in the eyes for the first time as he spoke to me. When he told me I would have a remarkable life I truly believed him. He never showed me such love before that day or after it. Actually that moment with Papa alone, burned the day on my memory.

Our moment came to a close as our guests began to gather for breakfast. And then Marlowe came into the room. He was still as he held my gaze. Before I could make it over to him breakfast was served. How lovely breakfast is but how sad I was at the idea that Marlowe was distant from me. We had become so close that summer and I began to fear that he did not want to marry me. I was devastated and did not eat. I had some tea.

When breakfast was over everyone gathered in the music room again. I just stood by the window looking out at the sea. My whole world would shatter if Marlowe did not want me for his wife. As these sad thoughts ran through my sixteen-year-old mind I felt him take my hand. He took my left hand in his and kneeled right in front of me ... in front of our guests and family members. He looked at me with so much adoration that I couldn't breath, I was forced back to the end of his eyes. "Nerissa will you do me the honor of becoming my wife?" Tears welled as I stared at him. Then all of a sudden I remembered that everyone was watching us. I looked up desperately to catch my father's eyes, which subtly smiled but also seemed lost in thought. I felt the air become thick. All I could say was "yes, of course, yes!" That was a magical moment in my life.

As the day proceeded, the wedding was planned. The most romantic wedding in history was to be prepared and had in two weeks time. September first would be our wedding day! A ball would be thrown that evening ... a delicious masquerade ball!

On that day I wore my skye blue dress with the whitest lace. I wore my pearls. I was beautiful and joyous. From that summer on I always referred to the day before our summer ball as the "skye blue" day. We shall not have a ball this year.

NERISSA

22 August 1911, somewhere in the middle of the night

Dear Diary, I woke choked by the stench of whisky. Our chambers were suffocating me in my sleep. I roused myself to ring for one of the girls to clean his preparation to writing. In that moment I longed to paint. I thought to myself, if he can disappear into the night with his words than I can do the same with my images. Sleeplessness always makes me crave the familiarity of it, for to work delivers me to myself and only after am I eased. I have a purpose and do not question my torments. As usual my tossing and turning is always met by his absence and it is like a competition to create. Knowing he is on the cliff inspires me to paint at night.

I sat to light the bedside candles so that I could dress and gather my tools when I saw our chambers.

Shame swelled inside of me as I looked at my destruction only half remembering. Through the darting light I caught glimpses; his armoire was lying on the floor empty and his desk no longer had his life on it. As I looked past it I saw his papers scattered all over the floor.

And then humiliation: I was crying as I ran into the breakfast room. All I saw were eyes, scared and bulging. I stood there by the doors and said, "You must all pack immediately." Whisper, whisper, whisper ... about my dress, the scissors in my hand, the streaks on my face ... I began to circle the table and as I did that I pushed the back of each chair as I challenged saying, "leave, leave, leave ...." Getting no response, "I want all of you to go home ... go back to your homes and leave me in mine. Are you deaf ... go!!!" With that, I began to swipe the china and food from the table. I must have broken some because I have cuts on my hands that sting.

My mother started to cry. I went up to her face and reprimanded her. "Stop crying Mama. Stop it now ... today is no longer a day of mourning. I will not allow this!" She wouldn't stop so I began to hit her. "Get out of this house; go now ... leave ... I can't bear the sight of you!" As I lashed out at her someone powerfully grabbed my shoulders from behind. When I felt hands trapping me I immediately swung my arms back to protect myself. They made contact with my Father. In that moment I felt his recurring betrayal as his arm came down on me with a force that knocked me to the floor. I tried to stand up but began to weave a bit and stumbled to the wall. They were cowering in their pretty little dresses and ties. As I tried to maintain some dignity I muttered, "All of you leave ... get out of my home ... I don't want any of you here." I could hear Mama whimpering. When I looked up I saw my father's face. "Especially you! You can't possibly understand my needs!" When I tried to stand up I almost tripped on the skirt of my dress. I hadn't cut it off completely. As I stumbled to the door of the dining room my father came up to it to block me. He was swift. Usually I would have been afraid, but this time I had fire in my brain. I had to get rid of everything in the castle that reminded me of Marlowe. I couldn't bear the sight of any of it. I didn't even look Papa in the eyes as I tried to clumsily push past him. "You are not leaving this room!" he said to me. That was all I had to hear to become hysterical. I began to pound on his chest through my vulgar sobs, "Let me go, I can't look at any of your faces, I can't look at anything that reminds me of Marlowe! Crispen! Odette! You must help me to clean the castle! We must get rid of all of Marlowe's things!" As my father had me cornered there my mother came up to soothe me. A force so strong broke out in me and as I knocked my father aside I ran out in the main hall. I disappeared up the stairs and though I was stumbling I kept running.

When I got to our chamber doors I began to cry harder than I have since your death. I felt like my ribs were breaking; my heart was pushing through them. I burst through those doors with such anger. I blamed you for all of it, for leaving me alone, trapping me with the fools that litter our lives, all of it. I hated you for giving up, for not letting me soothe your pain that night. I hated you for letting me fail you!

I went to our bed and tore the linens off. Dragging them behind me I threw open the windows that overlook the sea and threw them out. I could barely see anything. As I flung open the dressing armoire I reached in only to grasp your smell at the nape of my neck. Oh god, I collapsed right there tangled in your clothes. As I forced myself to stand I felt like I had to teach myself to walk again. Each step to the windows was painful; my legs felt swollen. I knew that throwing your clothes away would mean that I was losing another part of you and yet I wanted to rid myself. Article by article I threw you away. In a rage, so foreign, I kept going back for the rest and watched each item sink in the water. As I watched you disappear I knocked all your papers from your desk. There was a full bottle of whiskey on it and I smashed it all over your words.

Loving you the way I do doesn't make this pain worth it. Mumbling curses I fell asleep.

Oh, how sensitive animals are ... the cat has crawled onto our bed. She is purring quite loudly and is so very warm. Her black hair feels like silk against my naked skin. I wish I could disappear into her coat. Vanish into the depth of her black fur and curl into a ball there as she has done on my belly. She seems so content in her world. How pathetic I am to lie here motionless like a baby. Scribbling, scribbling, scribbling. Blanche reminds me of what I am not. I am not at peace. I am not still. The only time I ever feel as still as she is was when we touched or when I paint. I know that I have not yet become a real painter. I've only tasted moments of greatness. Unforgettable outbursts of truth. I work everyday either on canvas or in these pages and I long to work, but, am only beginning to break the chains of my mind ... thought. Only recently am I painting my heart nakedly without restraint. I learned from you that it takes tremendous courage to be an artist because when you create you are not your self anymore and know only the swelling of your soul and there are times when this tender nature could crush you and pull you under. But, you did it. I do it too, because I have to. I have to paint. I must go there and lose myself in those spacious moments. I have to become the lines around a woman's mouth when she smiles or the soft look in someone's tired eyes. I must lose my identity to the language of a person's face and the curve of the earth's body.

Loving you M. is similar ... you are the paint that let's me breathe my truth. There is no thought in loving you. I responded to you like nature exists. My love, you were every constellation in the sky for me ... you were the wet grass under my bare feet and all other things that feel good in nature. You were everything enormous and creative. For, everything grand I had experienced through you. When you touched me ... oh, how those feelings. . . when you touched me. All I could feel was the air thick around us. Your experienced hands would wash away all else and I was yours. They would travel my thigh and slowly find their way to my breasts. Your mouth silenced me as it discovered my lips. Kissing my neck and then the tenderness of my body, your hands would hold me in space and one cupped the small of my back and the other went deep inside. Your fingers would open me and play me masterfully. I could feel all the pages you had ever written and all the experiences you had ever had as you stroked me. As you touched my core I would feel you throb temptingly close to me like a heartbeat and gently you would find your way back. Always caressing my face ... you would hold it in your hands and when I looked into your eyes time took an enormous breath.

I remember the first time we made love. It was the night before our marriage. I was so scared I would fail you ... not please you. For I knew you had been with many other women in Paris ... experienced women.

Everyone was asleep in the castle. I had been sleeping restlessly in my bedroom when I saw the door timidly open. You watched me ... you thought I was sleeping. Then you walked gently into my room and stood by my bed. You sat by me and started to stroke my hair. The words you bestowed on me that night were both frightening and yet the most romantic words I had ever heard. As I lay there watching you speak I felt alive. Your face was so earnest as you promised to protect me for my whole life. "No one will ever hurt you again. We would be separate and safe in our unity." I listened as you told me stories about your past and how everything you had done in your life had meant nothing until that moment. You told me that you had loved me since the first moment you laid your eyes on me. I didn't know how to handle your sternness so I would giggle. You then became silent as you pushed the covers down to my waist. You looked at me ever so slowly as you unlaced the collar of my dressing gown. Touching my hot neck you leaned your face to my skin and began to kiss my collarbone, my ears and my hair for too long. Then you genuinely asked, "Is it alright?" I nodded my head. "This is because I love you Nerissa." I wanted to be with you and although it wasn't the proper time I knew I was to be your wife and so I said "show me how to please you."

You picked me up in your hands and gently stood me by the bed. After you took my dressing gown off, you told me to stand by the window so that you could look at me. I was quite unsettled by the rush of my feelings. The longer you looked at me the more I swelled. Marlowe, my love, you came to me and then you put your hand on the small of my back and let your other hand smoothly crawl across my belly, then to my breast and holding me like this you placed your mouth to mine and kissed me. My body was burning as I stood there awkwardly letting you touch me but I was scared and kept my hands by my side. I didn't know how to reciprocate. You then got on your knees in front of me and rested your head on my belly. With your arms around my waist, you held me like that for some time. "I love you angel," you whispered. I was more present in that room than I had ever been in my own life. Every nerve in my body was alert. . . breathing heavily, nostrils flared and temple throbbing; my body responded to yours.

As you held me like that you told me that you would show me all the beauty and magic in the world and that you would devote your life to my journey. I had tears in my eyes ... half from fear and half from joy. You had always been the one to guide me, not my father and I was yours and yours alone. Your words awakened some knowing and for the first time I moved my own muscles. I wanted to please you. I began to stroke your hair and press your face firmly onto my skin. God how I loved you. Then, for the first time in my life you touched my swollen lips with your tongue and took me completely in your mouth. You lit me. So, I said it ... teach me what to do. You told me to lie down on my belly, which I did. Engulfed in the air of us it felt too long before you touched me again. I know you were watching me and I loved the attention ... I loved being unsure in your presence because I knew that when you showed me the way it would be beyond all wonderful things I had ever experienced. When you came to me you first kissed my back, my legs, my arms. I could do nothing but accept your caress! Then you turned me over to face you and showed me how to make love. You told me to let my body enjoy all that would feel foreign ... I did and although it hurt and was terrifying in moments I knew I was experiencing something tremendous with you: my first lovemaking. I remember crying and I remember bleeding and I remember wondering if I would become pregnant. When the night sky had become a shade lighter you spoke of how I would be your wife and that there would be no more nights alone after that one. Then you left and I was in the silence of my childhood room with its many memories. All those silly girlish memories ... they seemed to be far in the distance. I had become a woman.

All that I have become is because of you ... your touch, your words, your thoughts have shaped me. As I lie here in our dark bedroom with such guilt I long for you. I want to look at the sea in the morning as we did together and feel it rise and fall within me. I want to wander into the kitchen when they are baking breads and lose myself in the warm aromas, lie in front of the fire in the library with my many books and travel those distant lands with the writers that seem like friends to me. I hope that living can consume me again and that with artistry I can turn my awe back onto the world, for those who have not been blessed enough to have loved and been loved.

I feel medicated from shame. Looking at the plum sky and at all of the stars I am pacified. Up there dancing with them I do find some kind of peace at last. Yet, there in the sky, boundless, I recognize myself hiding in the many corners of my life. I see myself small and terrified, nothing like the stars anymore! But, I do wish it! I want to live again. As I look back at our chambers and see Marlowe's papers I know I must paint ... that is my life now.

I know that I can be courageous through my work. Like Marlowe's friend, Mary Cassat, I must apply myself to the paintings. She has the bravery I lose sometimes. If I live for my work as she does I will find my map. I must always have the power to paint. That is my cure. Stroke by stroke I will soothe my soul.

I shall sleep again ... I love you M.

22 August 1911, Dusk

The day, somewhat intangibly, went by like mist. Exhausted from the past days and estranged from everyone here I ate alone and went for a long ride. I did not paint. I have failed myself as usual.

Goodnight M.

P.S. I thought of something today ... I am more frightened to remarry than I am to be a widow at twenty-one years of age.

23 August 1911, dawn

It is the loud breaking of my feelings that tires me; the high tide, the seasonal violence.

I have all the restlessness that was within him inside myself. The fear of fear. Yet, when he was alive I found serenity for his sake. I must have always worried for him. Now, there is no one to protect or a soul to be responsible to. Motherlessness. I have been drinking too much with supper because that is the only way I am finding some silence in my days. I empathize with his decision now, as I too wish to lose myself at the sea and never come back. Pulled under by salt-water hands that are relentless. I sit at the long dining table alone, sick with this desire: I want to drink too much one night and slip on the wet rocks. I am so tired. Why summons the energy to pretend I like being alive when I do not.

However I feel a responsibility to life, or is that God? I spend hours of life lost in the enormity of that question.

Living and death are larger and more significant than a moment or even many moments of isolated sadness. The beginning and the end of life is about everything unknown and either one can choose to honor and have faith in mystery or let the question overpower, driving one to rebellion against the unexplainable. On the other hand an equally unsavory option is living with a passivity that kills you as well. I was raised to believe in God. The question is about God. That is why and to whom I am responsible. I must continue steadfastly, not because of what I was taught in school, but because of my soul, my essence. As tormented as I am now it is my life passed from God's hands into bones and blood ... you, only you God are my explanation.

M. did not believe in God. We always differed in that.

Amen

24 August, 1911

I just remembered one specific morning. I was lighting a fire in our bedroom when Marlowe came up behind me.

I can still smell his heat. I can feel his skin soft from oils and salt. His hands rough. He easily claimed me and knew his way to me, for he had taught me my language and every aspect of my sexual expression. I wore him as my skin. We knew how to disappear into each other because our love making was a search for acceptance and when we pushed all boundaries physically, there was nothing in either of us that was misunderstood or unloved. We touched to win and we did. Because, for two people who never quite fit the world we fit each other utterly and belonged to something enormous and binding when we came together. Not much in life had ever made us feel that way.

Oh, I long to be touched.

There are many moments I remember. They surround me like breathing paintings. Moments floating in formaldehyde. I lose myself in each of them willingly ... find the tastes and smells that are so acrid. I feel the cold air around us when we were beyond temperature and discover where he would seduce me first. I taste his salty and damp body. I wonder if these moments torment him in heaven or if it is only the mortals that are left with memories that burn like vinegar. God, is it only the ones made of flesh and bone that cry themselves to sleep burdened by remembrances? Will I always suffer this?

Still, I wish to be stirred rather than coldly left with word memories: "I was Marlowe's wife." That means nothing to me when compared to remembering his essence poured on me. If I wander in our past and abandon reality, if I live with him although he is gone does that mean that I am delusional? Some say ill. Yet I am left with my deep intent: give me his smell, his touch, the sound of his voice and even let the tearing ache come, because the more vivid he is the less alone I am.

I miss you M., oh how I miss you!

25 August, 1911

I admit that we attract the things we obsess about. My life has been almost solely about loss.

When I was ten my best friend died, not physically, but mentally and emotionally. She was riding in a carriage with her older sister one evening when another one collided into theirs. Sarah Heller, my English friend, was knocked to the ground from the impact. The wheels of one of the carriages ran into her skull giving her a concussion. For one year, though she didn't speak, I waited for the possibility that she would laugh with me once again. I visited her everyday until I couldn't stand her not knowing who I was anymore. I remember telling her that I would come back the next day when I left that last night. I haven't seen her since. I often think about going by her home, but after being paralyzed by the climbing vines of years she is not the same person, nor

am I.

27 August, 1911

I've been lying here for quite a while with the Blanche, since before the sun rose, thinking about the future. If I am to survive I must discover my simple truths; filter them out. I suppose what I long for, above all else, is a genuine quiet that comes from constant growth. I've learned over time now that solitude is balm for my spirit. I should not stay in our chambers anymore. I am right in that. His presence is chaotic around me and I am paralyzed by it. Tonight I shall sleep there ... in clean bedding and begin to paint again. Oh yes, and I shall remember to eat today also. I should take better care of myself.

I need to bathe ... I wish mama could tend to me without driving me mad. She is insufferable ... either too frail or too strong with me. Neither is admirable. I find her to be the typical woman. She is an ancient scroll of woman. Neither has she written a deep thought nor painted an unforgettable moment. She spends all day dressing or entertaining. She is quite a bore ... everything I don't want to be. I cannot tolerate her trivial this morning.

Crispen is the only one left that understands me. As dramatic as he finds me at times I know that he empathizes with my need to be alone and work. He allows me to be withdrawn, just as Marlowe did, for he knows that on the inside I am active. Crispen is a craftsman, a man of the land ... of nature. He is a part of the rhythm of life and the earth here in Wick. I've watched him sitting quietly for hours in the same spot, staring into a distant point and I know he too is very much alive. He rocks in his chair, with his pipe and as I pass him by his glance says it all. "Hold tight child ... make peace."

Restlessness is what destroyed Marlowe. He could never slow himself. More than anything, what killed him was his passion ... it drove him to great highs and tremendous lows. He never was still. Even in my minds eye I feel him and his presence was like a constant flutter ... a baby bird that is ceaselessly trying to fly. His hunger for life killed him. I also live in that passionate place but long for peace. I don't know if I am capable, for every artist I know lives wontedly, but through this death I want to attempt it and try to learn from his mistakes. Truthfully, I am no better than Marlowe and willingly accept that I may fail. I realize living is a risk in itself. Yet I do believe I can find a calm within the emotional dishevel, some acceptance of the rise and fall of my psyche. I do desire to be wise as Crispen is.

Creativity and solitude are worth their risks. Art is all.

I shall ring for Crispen. Sometimes I wonder if he is even human. He seems translucent with his white hair and blue eyes. When he arrives I will have him send the girls to my old room with all its many windows. If there is a room to paint in it would be that one. This room was the loveliest room for writing, dark and melodious, but it is not meant for painting. For my work I need light and space.

28 August 1911, morning

I shall create a list of rules to be followed for I will need structure. A light meal before I work. I must paint in the morning before I bathe. Fresh water must be brought to me and the room shall be filled with canvas. If someone enters while I work I cannot be addressed as Miss. I require no formalities. After bathing I will eat a full meal. I will walk or ride west towards the Highlands alone after my lunch or travel with the servants into Wick to shop with them. One must learn where they are from. Although I am a mixed breed I do not feel French and need to stay acquainted with my land. After being in the fresh air I will have my tea and hours of stillness; dusk walks by the sea. Then supper. At night I shall have Crispen tell me stories of Scottish disposition and before I lay my head down to dream of you my love I will paint again. Discipline.

My existence will be so simple now. I am going to be able to dress myself without additional help because I am no longer going to wear the traditional clothing. I must only wear my dressing gowns. They flow and are free; white worn cotton with only a little lace. All those many formal gowns restrict me. I must have Odette order more from Paris.

Today I will live in an orderly way, holding the past at the length it should be. Now is not the time to remember ... to survive is to move forward; to do is to live, to wallow is to die. Tea, settling and my work! I can't say what the exact distance would but remembering years later is so much easier.

Oh, the cat is so warm on my belly ... but I must find the bell. I am tired of the sorrow that comes when there is no movement!

29 August 1911

How reckless this universe is. I know that is so. There may be a certain divinity to one's individual path but we all suffer. That is our commonality. I would never have imagined you wouldn't be here with me at this point in my life. Although you were seventeen years older and this of course meant the inevitability of you dying before me, I never looked that far ahead. To be here alone now is cruel ... truly a mistake has occurred. I suppose it affirms the fact that one never knows what the future holds or what senseless direction one will take. How could I have seen myself in this room, at the age of twenty-one, without you? Yet, here I sit. I notice the silence of no companionship and wish we'd had children. White is the color that holds you in this longing. Dreaming is almost as surreal as my life now. All is hushed. I've finished crying and throwing fits; I need not torment or be tormented. My muscles are exhausted and I am floating in a silent space of no feeling. I am sitting at the desk in my room with canvasses all around me that fog in and out of my consciousness. The steam from the tea is quiet too and the many family and friends still here seem sedate.

I find that I am in a peaceful state of shock now and am grateful to not be hurting anymore. All that is left is a vague ache, an empty cavity where you touched my soul. As I look out this window one thought crosses my mind: I wish I had painted you more often. I'd have so much more of you left for me. I want to see your face and find I have so little to refer to.

Looking at you explained my state of being. I would search for you only to know who I was because you silenced my performances. For the first time in our lives we didn't feel awkward and were truly vulnerable. My girlish insecurities passed because we two had a deep empathy. Now I will visualize you walking up behind me as I'm looking in a mirror or turn to what was once your place in the bed when I want physical love. I actively search for your image and struggle to find your presence so that I won't lose focus. And in those moments that are too short, I can see my map in your eyes and then with the crack of a belt it's gone. It is beyond my control and I have to experience losing you over again. I should paint you before memory no longer serves.

Your soul lingers around me and you seem to still be here somehow. It's as if you are in another room in the castle that I have lost the key to. I am in a limbo of still living with you and yet knowing you're dead. Your essence hugs my space with a heavy mist and in it I can smell you, hear you but I cannot touch you or see you.

I loved your laugh ... did I ever tell you that? I did ... so much ... I loved it and your voice ... the lines on your nose and by your eyes when you smiled. I was riveted when you walked into a room and felt bound to you. I belonged to you. How is it that your existence gave me such peace and I did not do the same for you? When did you stop believing I understood? I ache for not being able to fulfill you.

I'm sitting at this new desk surrounded by my childhood memories and yet I do not know where I am. Nothing fits me anymore. We redefined the meaning of everything. How strange it is to be in a place that used to be me but is no longer. This light room looks like another canvas to me. So different from where we slept; so different from our gothic room. It has no perspective yet. It will though and I suppose I should be excited by the idea of having a clean start but I am terrified. I am lost in the colors of my possibilities. On the desk lie all my freshly mixed paints. I love the way they smell ...bitter. Something in the scent of my materials wakes my mind.

The smell of it reminds me of coming rain or smoke from the chimney; familiar aromas that are like crawling into bed. My paint and my turpentine. As I look out this window I find myself passing like the clouds. This still place of numbness where you no longer live. I do believe now that I can survive this ... I can survive anything.

I will try not to think of your laugh or the smell of your warm hand as it touched my face. I will try so very hard not to want to run to you with each discovery. Darling, I will try. But, oh God how I miss you. There is ... there is only loss. I cannot imagine another mans hands on me.

I planned to read your diaries today but have determined to let them sit here in your leather folder until I am less sentimental. Did I ever tell you how incredibly gifted you were? You were my inspiration M. You were so much more to all of us than you had known.

Even Crispen, from his corners, learned from and admired you. He used to read your plays and poetry without your knowing because as he said to me, 'that he should keep you humble.' The only Marlowe he knew was the boy. Yet, he did admire you. Of course I doubt he ever told you his feelings but I know it to be true for I often found your works by his rocking chair. When I would mention it to him he would laugh his laugh, shake his white mane and his eyes would shine with a pride unlike any I had ever seen in either of our fathers. Maybe if he had told you.

Today is one of those gray, slow days where nothing amounts to much. Somewhat intangible. It won't even rain. I despise those days the most though. Nothing moves.

Oh M., morning alone is so different now that you're gone. No kisses.

30 August 1911

Dear Diary, I can bear days like this I should think. I kept to myself and had breakfast alone. I woke up at my normal time of seven and rang for tea and toast. Painted solidly for five hours. Exhausted by my work I had Odette bathe and dress me for my lunch and afternoon ride. There was a sense of direction and order.

I rode Lysiter and absorbed the damp horizon ... I let the colors carry me away and in that moment of galloping through the lush highlands. This country ... it is so rich! Paris never let me love it like Scotland does. It wants the praise of your eye. This is not unlike my horse. They too want your devotion. I've learned today that to care for others is a salvation. Marlowe carried me away from the needs of my childhood. Love again will sweep me into another chapter.

Lysiter is the first horse I've broken. I have a quiet understanding with him because of it and he is my muse to a certain extent. He craves my direction. And because my demands are read by him as his only language he shares in return a movement that knows me. Like today, he knew I was melancholy because after we had galloped and I had thanked him by leaning down to hug his neck he began to walk very slowly and repeatedly jerked his head to the left towards me. Well, I decided simply to not let myself think about any of it!

Sitting back up I clicked my tongue and nudged his belly. We galloped almost all the way back. I've cooled him now, untacked him and put his blanket on. He is in his stall with his neck leaned down to my head snorting and I am sure drooling from the apple I gave him. I don't mind. I just want to sit here leaning on his stall door for a little while. Sometimes there is no better place to hide then the stable.

My spirits are actually lifted and I almost feel that I would delight in some conversation. I may decide to have a formal supper with everyone. I might try to do that. Maybe Crispen will let me join him for dinner. That may be better.

30 August 1911, after a brilliant dinner with Crispen

He spent the entire evening making me laugh as he told me the most ridiculous stories about my childhood. Pirates ... I always wanted to play pirates! He told me about one evening in particular when I was five. I didn't want to move away to Paris so I hid in Crispen's room all day and night. Everyone was searching for me. First for lunch and then dinner. After the search had ended everyone worriedly retired for the evening. Crispen had come to his room to have some whiskey and to think further on where I could be. He said that suddenly, it dawned on him that I would often hide in his room when Marlowe and I would play Hide & Seek. So, he started to talk aloud to himself about how he would miss everyone and that the Ship had taken off safely after supper that evening. He told me that all he heard was "Crispen, have they really gone?" When he turned around he saw my red hair and dirty face sticking out from under his bed. He said "Aye Miss, they are off and away. Somewhere in the North Sea by now, I should imagine", I said, "Thank goodness because I have plans to stay here and be a Pirate!" Then I pulled myself out from under the bed, which I had difficulty with because I had a loaf of bread and a jug of water with me. Then I said, "I am going to sleep here if that's alright Crispen because real Pirates don't sleep with dolls!" He said, "Alrighty Captain!" and left me to sleep.

I had forgotten about my obsession with Pirates. How silly I was ...

Goodnight M.

1 September, 1911

Painted. Argued with my Father at dinner. We argue very well.

Papa finds sport in embarrassing me. It stimulates him. The one pleasant thing he said this evening was that he intended on "LEAVING WITH OR WITHOUT ME." I should have said, "I'm so sorry to see you go." But instead I took him seriously. I lose my sense of humor when it comes to him.

In truth I know he does love me and is only concerned to leave me alone in Scotland while I am grieving. I am fragile in his mind and he does not believe he can trust me. He is guarded as if I was a terminally defiant person set only on conflict never compromise. If I were a boy he would find me with strong character. As a woman I have a frail mental state and combative personality. He never gives me a chance to be pleasant.

He has to go back to Paris to finish building and has no choice but to leave. So, I said, "I do understand. You should work but I must be here with my husband." Of course my response was not logical so an argument, at high volume, ensued. Mama did not find a way to defend me. She has always chosen him above me. Yet, I do wish one day she would surprise us all and love her child above all else. That is the kind of mother I would be. She is an aristocratic female. A woman stuck in convention. They seem to have no thoughts of their own. Either she passively agrees with everything Papa says or she manipulatively insinuates what she would prefer. Besides she has always despised how much time Papa and I like to spend here. She desires to go and is irritated by this uncivilized country. She has always been jealous of his interest in me. I don't even know if she is intelligent. I do not know her. Even if she would show herself to me I do not know if I could understand her.

Therefore, supper once again was thoroughly disappointing and left me without an appetite. I excused myself by making some snide comment about his remarkable ability to excuse me from any room that he is in.

The only time we were ever able to enjoy each other was during my marriage. We would be at supper during this last summer and somehow I would end up discussing more with Papa than anyone else. He is really quite charming and for the first time in our lives together we found each other fascinating. I would pour him another whiskey just so he would not have to get up and leave the conversation. Because of the fact that I had a husband he was relieved of worry; it eased his mind that he did not have to tend to me anymore. I knew it gave him peace and I found it easy enough to forgive his shortcomings. You see I do believe Papa loves and sometimes even likes me. Yet, I think he has always had a difficult time being needed, especially by the ones he loves the most. He is most comfortable revealing himself to people he is not committed to; quite the social disease. Plainly, I think he is unaccustomed to a woman having her own thoughts that differ from his. He is, after all, a man. So, I suppose when he saw me with M. he found release from his guilt at having failed me and my unique needs. Now once again we oppose each other and feel awkward in the others presence.

All the pieces fit when I became M.'s wife. Now everything has changed. Still, do I fool myself with fantasy? Are my recollections true? I feel I had an incredible marriage that grew me from a girl into a woman, that I knew my husband better than anyone else, yet I don't know where we ended and his need to leave me began. That night ... oh, that night when I uncharacteristically slept too long. I imagine now that I must have slept deeply in our time together, otherwise I would understand why ...

3 September 1911

From the time I was a little girl Marlowe called me his "Angel". Ironically now he's mine.

4 September 1911

Dear Diary the sunset in Scotland is quite stunning to witness as it drifts. I am included in the many shades of white and gold ... low sky here. There is a gulf of color which turns pale blue when you blink your eye and then turns into night. I have been feeling rather strong again since my accident and have begun to finish the painting I had started on the day that I fell. An eternal stare. When I was a child and would visit for the summer I would stand here at our spot and wonder why one couldn't see all of Europe for truly one could see such a far distance. Marlowe often wrote there. It is a place where many of our memories were made, where we first kissed. It is that view of the water and horizon I am painting now. I also believe it must be the place where he drowned.

As I sit here at the end of a fine day's work to watch the sunset, I finally find some perspective. Humbled by God's enormity in the dashing yellows and whites that chase through the pale blue sky into the falling night I am silenced. I see my soul up there and all the answers to my longing questions. God has created both beauty and suffering for texture and as we descend through the layers of life we will learn the sought wisdoms. If we can sustain through our journey and not abandon ourselves or others for fear of hurting, nor let our senses become dull we will achieve the great bounty God promises. I will find my peace through faith. Humility is wisdom.

I know I shall sleep peacefully this evening.

Amen.

5 September 1911

Dear Diary,

Only now can I touch the wet open wound of both truths: the only being that I have ever trusted was not trustworthy and still he will remain rooted in my heart and as the air I breathe affect me daily. Reading his papers has, I feel I've been living with this for too long now as a secret shame I always knew but denied, exposed us and destroyed the allusive power I have always let him hold over me.

I was looking for a way out, a way to blame him and not myself for his death. In search of where he began his mornings and ended his nights I hoped to find a sadness that would redeem me from whatever guilt was aching in me.

I knew he had been decadent in Paris. I knew of whores ... all kinds of women; the late nights of opium. I wanted to read his thoughts about who he was during that time when he learned about how dark he could become and in that illumination I longed for confessions of destruction that might make the part of him I was not allowed to know more tangible. If I could discover the man who had lived without ethics I might be able to except his death and forgive us both. I have accepted his disappearance and am grateful for it now, because I've learned that we were imprisoned in our marriage. Although we loved we lived falsely and lied to each other everyday. I did find his edge as I read and read the night away. I revealed the most cutting fact, which is that we lived out a creative fantasy but never did achieve a transcendental love. I found the Marlowe that committed suicide and the me that couldn't stop it. I suppose whatever control I am trying to exercise now as I write of these events, logic still points to him. It can be his fault for now. I refuse to take responsibility for us because he was the adult. He married a child. What did he expect but a nursery rhyme of love? I have been released.

As for him he was sicker than any man I have ever known was.

He felt he was worthless and yet he seemed to believe he was beyond any of us. M. lost his mother during his birth and I knew that loss weighed on him heavily ... he felt utterly alone in his world and pined after her, Diedre Elspeth Sinclair. He suffered from the disease of blaming his father for not being in Scotland to save her and revered desertion as his cross to bear. Marlowe nurtured his isolation like someone continually picking a scab. He claimed to be a chosen one: tested by God with highs and lows that were beyond the average mans and given the intelligence and vision of the elevated. He hated God for it and felt forced to live in a place of such dichotomy that life seemed to be a meaningless torture.

Marlowe felt contempt for the world that read and watched his plays. Always misunderstood, he harshly judged their ignorance and lack of depth. Daily he was spiraling into a darkness that he felt trapped in and never shared with me. Yet, in his self-loathing, he despised his own cynicism (which is why he fell in love with me, for I was innocence personified. Rather than dissect the aspects of himself that manipulated his psyche he chose, instead, to to lose himself in his obsessions. It is sad, as his wife I feel this and yes also as a fellow artist, that he was his worst critic. Like ointment, sarcasm oozed from his own interpretation of the overuse of drugs and alcohol; his faithful lovers that were able to hush the many voices and help him escape his personal noise. M.

was consumed with the word distance. It rang. He had pages throughout his Diaries that would list words he loved. "Distance" was always amongst the others.

And that he did. He distanced himself from all of us. Nothing was longed for, not me nor art, above removing himself from his narcissistic pain.

There were so many mornings when he couldn't find his evenings yet, he felt comfortable and safe curled in that cloud of forgetting who he was. I am not saying I didn't know this about him. I did know his melancholia. Actually I understood it quite well and lived with my own torments. After all, as he so intellectually and objectively wrote, he did mold me. However, I also see the differences that must have glared at him. For although I know the darkness, I do have faith and ethics which illuminate my urge to find meaning. M. lacked control because he was a prisoner of his reality and had no perspective; faith was a myth. Belonging to nothing he couldn't stop himself in the name of anything or anyone. It destroys my love to think about where the he I knew began and ended. Did I know the monster and ignore his growls or did he methodically choose to share only a part of himself. Whatever the answer, there were secrets and I never did know the man I was supposed to mirror.

You see, Dear Diary, it is one thing to be consumed by life; ebb and flow with it's enormous tides and yet it is another to have it overwhelm you. He was weak. Tormented by feeling tremendously responsible to save others and yet contempt towards them as well was Marlowe's daily existence. If he engrossed himself in his work, in his addictions, his experiences and then in his love he did not have to face himself. He ran until he couldn't anymore. And although he contributed and gave to mankind, I find his terror, denial and judgement of God to be hypocritical.

Excepting that his love for me was an attempt at true love from his safely distanced vantage point is one of many aspects I am faced with now. He could not live, he had to manipulate everything he experienced with his theories because it helped him to remain removed. Yes, as an artist and a thinker he used me explore love's possibilities and captured my youth to recapture his lack of it. I was too young or too desperate for his approval to have ever exposed us and so I hid my intuition of this along with my other sadnesses. I needed him desperately because of his consistency; he had been the only person to dote on me. I too was addicted in a sense. The tragedy is that M. loved me deeply, more than anyone else. He could not become more intimate or real than he was with me. For that I pity him.

When I was born, Marlowe was more prolific than ever. But his writing changed dramatically at that point, his plays included. The new theme being the exploration of transformation and the forgiveness of sins. What was redemption and thus that mysterious noun: God? William Blake comes to mind. Much ink and pen became absorbed with me. He wrote of how I was helping him to see his whole future filled with the prospect of purity. His descriptions of children and what they represented for adults were profound. I can only imagine what a baby will do for my soul as well. He spoke of the preservation of innocence and was obsessed with the belief that one should control and mold their children so as to save them from the influences of the world. All that he seemed to believe in regards to parenting echoed eerily of my own marriage. I was inundated with his ideas, preferences and beliefs. He guided me and taught me all his truths about the world and art, made me care for people in a way that a little girl cannot naturally, yet always stressing my own independence. I never felt it was improper though. Quite the contrary, I was hungry for his experience and knowledge both as a child and as a woman. He had lived far more than anyone I knew had and I revered his style, intelligence and what I thought was pure dedication to his art. I loved M. and while I would listen most intently, I soulfully assumed I was also learning about him and not being censored a perception. I thought I knew him, which obviously I did not.

In his private thoughts I found such calculation. I spent my life around him and never knew what I was allowing him to do to himself and me. He believed that he was solely responsible for the woman I was. In fact, he thought he had created the perfect woman in me. His manipulation of who I was to become and who I had become excited him and he felt I was his masterpiece ... his lifelong work. I wasn't true love to him. I was a concept. And although Marlowe loved me and I him, he has stolen our purity away in those pages. He's raped me of my identity. Who am I, if I could be so mistaken about us?

My memories from the first five years of my life are fragmented. I mostly remember that I was most alive when I was alone or with him. There are recalled blurs with my parent's friends coming from Paris periodically to vacation at our estate; I see how tall they were as they stood before me when they arrived. I remember receiving colorful, sparkling gifts at supper, Odette bathing and reading to me, Crispen teaching me to pray. Smells are vivid like my mothers smoke and perfume as she readied herself in the mornings and evenings or the aromas from the cooking pantry where the ladies would prepare our meals. I don't recall children my age from that time, for I was either alone or with adults. So, although Marlowe sought me I was easily reached. I mainly sat off to the side observing the many eccentrics that littered my life. I watched them live. They did not know what to do with a child. Our circle was quite sophisticated; intellectuals and artists, many of who did not have children or whose children were already grown. My parents couldn't have been more awkward with me. So, because of all these elements I learned to depend on him. He made me feel interesting.

Loneliness breeds isolation, but isolation breed's creativity, so I learned to love imagination and thrived on entertaining myself. My time with him was filled with that dappled magic: storytelling, hunts in the house, riding and games in the gardens. He showed me

Scotland ... the Highlands ... and I would come home at lunch for my soup and bread with a cold face, exhilarated from playing out of doors. Through time spent with Marlowe I became inquisitive, creative and generally complicated. It was a rare time of both a sweet childishness and a pre-mature awareness. I was fascinated by life and quite aware of my fascinations. This is what I remember on my own.

    I have always been grateful to Marlowe for being a brother to me when I was a little girl; caring for me and spending time. All I experienced was colored with his uninhibited interpretations. As an adult I have had the courage to look back and digest the sadness I felt then for having parents that didn't know how to love me and very much have felt thankful that someone cared about my well being and my development. Mainly, in a world filled with intellectuals and artists who smoked, drank and slept late I have been grateful to Marlowe for giving me a childhood. He made the unusual exciting. Now he has taken what memories I do have and corrupted them and embarrassed me. The innocence of where we began is obsolete now.

I am devastated to be feeling such contempt and blame towards the one person who could do no wrong and yet I struggle to find any other sane reaction to the things I've read. I was simply another obsession he could distract himself with. My soul was opium. In his diary I found one passage that truly has disturbed me about our marriage.

"I believe quite thoroughly that life is what you make it. We are bound to suffer and accomplish nothing unless we claim our creative power. I am nothing out of the ordinary, in fact, I find myself to be rather weak and typical. Yet, my life is a masterpiece filled with exciting people who will be remembered in our histories. I am a published writer at the age of twenty-two and have found public acclaim. If the truth were known, I did not start out having some Godly type gift. I have worked and

worked at finding my eloquence and voice. I am capable of enduring and materializing anything! So, I find that it is because of my desire to fill a certain role that I am who I am. I have created my existence like a painting.

Maybe true love is the same. Maybe it does not exist. Possibly, it is simply an idea one sets out to fulfill. Usually one passively wishes for something, instead of actively assuming the responsibility of the result. This is because people are afraid to ask the right questions. They are afraid to believe love does not exist so, they keep searching rather than saying: It shall be. I shall have this person and they will be this way ... the way I anticipate.

Nothing in this world amounts to much. I, in my peculiar universe do not amount to much. I am a self-absorbed, bitter and brooding man. Yet, I prove to myself how correct I am in my estimation of control when I observe, as I said, my writing for instance. I have turned my simplicity into gold through effort. I am beginning to believe a man should be with a much younger woman so that he can mold her into what he wants his "true love" to be. He could grow her. Why believe in anything other than yourself. Hasn't everything failed you at least once? Nothing and no one will bring you peace. Everything I possess will come from me."

Our existence is completely circumstantial. All that I have learned has been colored by my translation. I except both that M. manipulated us but, that he loved. In fact, he did so deeply that the pain and disappointment that is inevitable in this life became too overwhelming for him. You see, as an artist, I can comprehend the pain of seeing and feeling too much. Everything has a resonance; every smile, face and country and all the elements that make up this world. He was a deeply hurting individual that believed nothing particularly magical could come to him without effort. Ultimately, that is why he killed himself ... he became tired of the continuos effort to make his life special. I think even his love for me exhausted him. I must have taken up too much of him. I know that M. loved me more than anyone else in the world. But, Dear God it has taken me time to believe that again. Yet he did, with all his intensity and passion. He loved me with a power capable of beginning and taking life.

Although I resent the impression he had of himself on me he was right in some ways. He did "grow" me and I did become a woman with him. In many ways he is the one and only person who has truly known me and I him ... how sad for us. He may have accomplished much of what he set out to but, he was a master manipulator, a dark and distant man who received far too much power over me.

I realize now, that his being gone is a great relief and will give me a freedom I've never had.

Yet, in the morning when I wake expectant of his touch, I quite simply miss my husband. It is the morning now actually. I can hear the echo of absence as the wind blows through and around our home. The air seems stale within these walls. Everyone but the help has left and they are too timid to talk to me. They pass me in the halls with their heads down ... "Good Morning

Miss." The loneliness is unbearable at times and makes me long for the reassurance of M.'s presence. If loneliness were a person it would be the most seducing of women ... a gypsy dancing you away from yourself. Mornings are made of fantasy now, as I long for a man who has humiliated me and soiled the memories of what was once a fairy tale. I should put my efforts into making up with my family. Thank God for Crispen. Oh, the Doctor is coming to see me ... I should wash up.

7 September, 1911

Dearest Diary, it is a quarter past four in the morning. I am sweating and cramping. It feels as if someone's hands are swimming inside my stomach. I wish Odette would come tend to me and yet I'm exhausted and only want to fall asleep again. Too many restless night's.

Soon I will have to write Papa about my condition, for he and our guests will be arriving for Christmas. I suppose Doctor MacLachlan might have already written to them, though it's doubtful. They would have contacted me immediately if they knew. Will they be pleased?

NERISSA

8 September 1911, sometime before dawn

Dear Diary, I thought my nightmares would end. Yet, I still wake thinking he is alive. When will he stop haunting me? His visits at night are rich in detail and have elements of horror. I must know more about the traveling I do when I sleep. My dreams as my thoughts are exhausting and transporting; real as living being. I wonder, somehow, if I do go to M. It is most certainly not the first time I have woken to a vivid sense of psychic awareness. Images that tell me of places I've never visited or events that have yet to transpire but that will take place. I've seen proof in the past. My dreams have pushed me into the future long before I was prepared for circumstances to occur. My dreams are not unlike my marriage; elements that force me to accept what has yet to become. If I look back now I know that I was his before I was sixteen. I was his the day he thought of me as his project and possession. His mere thoughts catapulted me into a premature adulthood. And in a similar way at night I have been exposed to divorce and death good fortune and love before the actual events occurred. Do I find M. on an astral plane between heaven and earth?

9 September 1911

I have no words to describe the rage I feel towards the society we live in. I received a letter from Gerald, who has informed me that he would be honored to exhibit my work under one condition. He recommends that I take a masculine name. He suggests it easily as if it is so common that I should not mind at all. I couldn't help but laugh at his audacity ... the world's audacity.

I've been thinking of the lists of female artists who have not been taken seriously and fear he may have a significant point; that I will not be taken seriously as Marlowe's widow who is living an eccentric life of solitude in Scotland. However, if I was thought of as a man who was purely reclusive and has no interest being known by the public I will seem intriguing. Being a man changes the entire perspective of one's way of living. It's pitiful that when passions are exhibited in a woman's nature they are seen as inappropriate. How can my breasts diminish my colors? How can they think this logical? A person's ability to capture light and emotion is not contingent upon what is between their legs!

Women, like Mary, who never married are looked at suspiciously. People are afraid to tread to close to these unusual creatures! It astounds me that society can still look at men and women and not comprehend the inevitable human similarities. I wish to avoid this confrontation with ignorance. Also, I must admit here secretly, my need for recognition sways me. I want to be accepted as a legitimate painter and I resent existing in the shadows of men. Yet, being the wife of Marlowe I am too aware of what this perpetuates.

I cannot make this decision today.

12 September 1911

It is night and I cannot sleep. A memory has surfaced. I am ashamed for him.

I was thirteen when I began to paint. Marlowe insisted to my parents that oil painting lessons would be very nurturing for my adolescent mind, making me more creative than other children. M. would write me long letters at this time about art and it's importance. He would explain that the exploration of ones quiet places is what must be painted and was firm about the discipline I should exercise in discovering my unique expression. Seek and then listen ...

His letters for the most part were beyond my reach.

Yet, as Marlowe often was, he was right and I did begin to mature ahead of my classmates. I can see it now when I look at those old paintings. There was one of Sarah riding a horse; galloping wildly underneath her, she without saddle was riding him bareback with the skirt of her dress carelessly and unabashedly exposing her legs. Their hair blowing recklessly in the wind showed their speed. Both slightly wet from splashing through a Loch; bare feet and muscles defined from squeezing the body of the horse between her. Nothing stated and yet an awareness and sensuality unusual in someone that age.

It is true, that I can recall a preciousness in my fourteenth year. Yet, my intentions, like the metaphors of my paintings, were naïve. I did not know the effect I was having on men. Actually, I think I was only duplicating what I watched older women do. All the while, I enjoyed the attention I would receive from standing too close or hugging for too long and then suddenly moving on as a child does.

My painting instructor Cassel was a friend of Marlowe's and wrote to him about my flirtations and his desire to have me. He told Marlowe of the way I would lift my skirts up and spread my legs on either side of the easel while I painted. I knew he was looking and that my lack of formality drove him mad, but I had no awareness of the power of a man's longing. I did not know my affects. My own desires were vague and I had no words or ways to express them for I did not even know they were that. I merely felt the sensations from spreading my legs, closing and opening them to feel the cool breeze that would rush through the languid studio. I knew the warm glow when I would wake in the morning and squeeze the hot covers in between my thighs.

Marlowe wrote to me at that time. He suggested a new instructor that he thought was better and now I know why. When I wrote back that I liked Cassel and did not wish to change he must have taken this as a terrible sign.

Marlowe came to Paris earlier than usual that year. I remember him taking me to a café for lunch in the middle of my lessons where he talked to me of love and passion. Asking me about my opinions and boyfriends he finally asked me if I had let Cassel touch me. I had no answers to his questions and started to laugh because I was embarrassed by his words that were beyond me. He took my laughter as a sign of guilt and began to become quite upset with me. He told me that good girls did not do such things at my age. He began to tell me about lovemaking and what he wished I would experience in my womanhood. He spoke to me like an enraged Father, or so I thought. Finally, when he finished his monologue, I asked him why he was telling me all of this. He said that Cassel had told him about my naive advances and his shameful desire to pursue them. I assured Marlowe that nothing had happened. I also remember telling him, indignantly, that he should save his lectures for another girl, that I was not a child and had mature feelings of my own. I did not really know what I was talking about but I hated being treated like a little girl when I did not feel that way. "I had woman feelings." He looked me steadily in the eyes and said, "Not yet you don't." He took me back to school and we never spoke of it again. My lessons with Cassel ceased although I do not believe Marlowe told my parents anything other than that Cassel was too busy to instruct me. Marlowe stayed in Paris until I finished my studies. He watched me like a guard and attended all the Balls with me ... I was never out of his sight. We argued that winter and spring. Then, he escorted me back to

Scotland for my annual summer visit, which he had never done before.

When I read M.'s Diary's I found his true impression of that time. Beyond words was his jealousy. The discoveries I made in those pages ...

When his friends began to arrive for the summer festivities he saw the way the men took me in. He watched the way they responded to my walking past them. It drove him to anger that they too would look at my young face and then lose themselves in my overdeveloped body. I had breasts, long legs and childbearing hips that did not belong on a fourteen-year-old. I did not know any of this at the time ... I was just a girl who had spirit. I loved people and found it easy to be intimate yet knew not the impact I had. Although I was beginning to feel certain things they were not as developed as my body and the flirtations were as innocent as any game I might play. But Marlowe's reality of this time was irritated and filled with frustration. He wanted to be with me, yet was ashamed of his longing. All this I have to digest now ... it leaves me half-sick and yet I tenderly miss this man who has loved me so desperately all my life. And I have learned from this loss how crucial being desired is for the soul.

He, who knows me better than anyone, saw me grow from a child into a woman and loved ... how can I condemn him for that? Is Love not Love? Why does age or circumstances change the purity and depth?

Yet, it does ... it does.

Now I lay me down to sleep, I pray the Lord my soul to keep. If I must die before I wake, I pray the Lord my soul to take ... Amen.

13 September, 1911

Today I took a rather challenging ride with Crispen. I will not be able to for much longer due to Doctor MacLachlan's urgings. He worries I'll fall and miscarry. I've decided I am excited about being a mother now ... it just took me some time. I quite simply was disturbed by the idea of raising M.'s child, but, I've realized this isn't about him anymore. It's about us; we're the one's that are still alive and we are family. The question had to become about my desire to be a mother and not about who the father was. When I clarified that for myself the answer was a profound yes. On our ride we talked about baby names.

It was one of those days that seemed to hold still on gray, and yet from time to time the sun would break through the clouds and radiate with hollow lines. The shifting between the clouds and sun was brilliant and the light today was iridescent. I must paint it.

As we rode we talked of many other things. We had one of those unusual talks about everything and it lasted for the entire afternoon. For the first time I saw Crispen as a man and not a God. I saw sadness in his eyes and wondered why he had never been married. I asked and when he told me he had, I felt ashamed that I hadn't known. He told me that she had died in childbirth before I had been born.

Crispen has always worked for my father's family. In fact, our families went back together for at least three generations on the West Coast near the Isle of Skye. Papa and Crispen were raised alongside each other and had been friends for most of their childhood. When they were nineteen their paths diverged as childhood friendships do and often stature forces. Crispen fell in love and married a girl named Kristy Lenox. She was the love of his life and when she became pregnant he knew what true happiness was. Those eight months were the richest of his life ... flawless. He talked about watching her grow, feeling her hot body change, of joy and pride. He told me about all these new sensations I can expect to have soon. For the first time someone I cared for truly empathized with me and it was deeply soothing. All I could do was listen as this man who seemed untouchable by grief shared with me a pain he had carried and I had never known. She had died in childbirth and the baby as well died inside of her. She had been too small and frail to endure the trauma. That was it ... in a flash Crispen's light was snuffed out. Here he was forty odd years later all alone. He had never remarried and for some reason I had never questioned his solitude until now. I felt truly selfish as we rode along the water this afternoon. I had not cared enough about this man who had raised me like a Father to wish to know about his own life. On those many nights when Mama drank too much and was still enjoying her crystal-shattering laughter and talking about everyone else's character it was Crispen who would put me to sleep, read to me, and reminded me to always pray. He has been my center and yet in ways I have treated him like a servant; only interested in how he could entertain and protect me ... children can be cruel. I am not a gracious person and was ashamed to recall that our talks over the past two decades have focused on me and not at all on him. Thank you God for this old man who has given me what values I do have.

We were outside so long that we had the joy of watching all the gray and all the sun get swallowed by night like a enormous whale catching it's last breath before diving under. I love nightfall. It puts everything into perspective when you witness God's miracles.

P.S. I feel quite confident of my plans now. The Scottish cannot be fenced in, must not be afflicted by someone else's rules. No matter how much French blood I have in me I am Scottish. The recent turn of events with regards to my work will not stop me from breaking into their world and I will do it my way whether I take a masculine name or not. We will remain here despite what others may say. Crispen said it also; it is important for our child to be where Marlowe's spirit still lingers. For me it will be difficult but to grow into a person of distinction our child must live the way we have lived. Smelling the sea everyday and wandering in the Highlands creates a sense of awe that any great person must have. Imagination; nothing is more colorful than

Scotland. This land is one of loyalty and passion. Bones in earth that make the standing strong.

If it is a girl I shall name her Sheila (we could use some music in this home now). If it is a boy I will name him Bruce after my father.

Goodnight Marlowe, my love.

17 September 1911

I have a confession. I do not know for sure how Marlowe would have felt about my pregnancy. It was odd that, for a man his age, he never spoke of wanting children. Because of how young I was in our time together I'm sure his intention was to not rush me out of my own childhood. I do desperately hope that up there he is a happy Father; that he is happy, above all else, for the manifestation of our love and not some perverse stroke of luck in me carrying on his legacy. He couldn't have choreographed it better. Only a mind like Marlowe's would think such a thing and only a mind like mine would feel compelled to question the illogical.

What a pair we two made. I create obstacles for myself and with others. Shadows is what he would call the feelings that ate away at me.

Still, I wish I could have seen his reaction when I found out that morning. I am going to choose to see him as very pleased. Although I have exposed his private thoughts he was not a malicious and cruel person. He had a very big heart and probably would have made an excellent father much of the time. He was a great one to me. Another confession: a part of me was looking for a father in him from the very beginning. He filled my own holes as well and cannot be the only one to blame. From here forth I will take some more responsibility for my own contributions. M. was right about the fact that we can enhance our existence by believing and willing things to be a certain way.

18 September, 1911

As I look thee in thy eye, I see mine own reflection and beg the answer for why I drain my soul with evenings of discontent and mornings of regret. By my heart, I swear to not undo you my sweet with the sorrow that eats away at me. Now, with you growing up in Paris I find myself alone and see how little I deserve thee. Though I do, I do; I plead to have the gentle heart to be loved by a woman as innocent as you. That my life has not been taken from me is a wonder. For I am cruel. My existence is a gift I hold in the lowest regard. With regret, I beg forgiveness from everyone who has found the foolishness to love me. I see you kneeling Angel, by a pool of tears that I fear will be my doing. With that fantasy I am again ashamed by my selfishness. I feel no elation or pride in this, my life. I also kneel, pitifully; promising justice to the God's by swearing to never let another love me. All of this is truth and yet I desire you, I long for your warmth. Beyond the self-loathing, beyond my convinced notion of undeservedness, I know you to be my reflection. Eyes that have not seen the world as of yet, they redeem me of my destruction. They rescue what little is left of my good heart. In your face I see all my potential for beauty and humility. I have waited almost a lifetime. Though I am wrongful in offering my years to you, I can imagine no more time without thee, my true love. Forgive me for loving you.

Yes this is what haunts me. To read his private diaries ... to be referred to as the lover he had always longed for when I was only nine years old has been devastating.

19 September, 1911

The decision has been made. I will do as Gerald advises and assume a masculine name in order to be seen and to have an impact on the world. Yes I will abandon titles for my sense of accomplishment. I will betray my womanhood. I must write to him in Paris. Privately though, more than any other feeling, I seethe with anger. I would never wish for anyone to read this but I envy man. They have many less challenges than we do and I crave to see the world through a mans eyes and have the world respond to me in turn. Their independence alone makes me wish to trade. Yet, as I feel this baby growing inside me and I think of the love I shared with Marlowe, when I think of the soul of woman ... simply that, then I recognize, at the core of my soul, my femininity. I know I shall live with remorse though. For although I have not betrayed myself and the women who created me in my heart, I have betrayed us nonetheless.

2 October 1911

I hear the sounding entrance of my Faith in God. All joy and pain is the sum of me and as I apply myself to loving that which I am, Faith knocks with piercing and unwavering clarity. I do not presume to have passed through Mourning but I honor my reverence to this life...my walking meditation. On my knees, as my heart flutters with the wings of angels, I see God. I bow my head.

Amen

Notes from Estelle Lochalsh

My great-grandfathers Bruce Strachan Weymss and Angus Ronan Lochalsh were childhood friends and both from wealthy West Coast families in Scotland. Together they were sent to complete University in Paris where they similarly graduated under the title "Architect". When their parents died they returned to Scotland to sell their family estates and decided to purchase a castle in the Northern Highlands that overlooked the sea where the Atlantic meets the North. They wished to live in Paris to enjoy the pursuits of their Firm but spent summers in Scotland. The Wemyss-Lochalsh estate would become their life long project and all of us associated with it their life long dream.

The summer that they came home and began the restoration Angus married his childhood love Deirdre Elspeth Sinclair. Deirdre became pregnant with a boy named Marlowe Caesg Lochalsh but died during the birth. Angus never completely recovered from the loss and therefore never remarried. After this tragedy, Father and newborn Son boarded a train back to Paris where they joined Bruce. Eventually Bruce married Genevieve Charlotte Demarchier and despite the age difference they reportedly were passionate about each other. They married in France but shortly there after moved to Scotland where they remained for six years. Genevieve immediately became pregnant with a girl named Nerissa Jacqueline Wemyss Lochalsh. Marlowe's life proved to be rather exciting and he became published while in University. He was quickly embraced as a poet and playwright and infamous as a man.

 In 1890 due to Genevieve's pregnancy, Angus' illness from pneumonia and Marlowe hitting an all-time low with drugs Marlowe and his father traveled back to Scotland for a much needed rest. The two families that through friendship were one lived together in Scotland for five years. Genevieve tried to take care of her daughter and husband but spent much time missing the high society of Paris. She was young and relied on her servants. Although Nerissa flourished in the Scottish countryside it all came to an end when Angus and Bruce were commissioned to build a train-station in Paris. Nerissa, Genevieve and Bruce traveled back to France. Angus and Marlowe stayed in Scotland because of the illness. Seven months later Angus died. The death drove Marlowe over the edge. Every fall when he would travel to Paris with his latest works that he had completed during the summer he was notorious. He suffered serious addictions and spent time in opium and whore houses. Of course he would see Nerissa, as well as his Aunt and Uncle but he never failed to put aside many hours for self-destruction. Eventually he would always find his way back to Scotland for the winters once again.

Nerissa and her parents would also return as promised every year for the whole of the summer. Since his Father's death Marlowe had created an annual event where he would invite approximately thirty artists to Scotland for two weeks. He would use those weeks as inspiration for his latest work. When a guest arrived they would be escorted to their chambers where there would be a card describing who they were, i.e. their social status, physical uniqueness, their nationality, time of year, sexual preference, health status ... 'their character'. In the wardrobe would be the appropriate clothes for such a character. For one week everyone would mingle under those false identities. Marlowe would use the improvisations he witnessed as kindling for his work. Amongst the players were Degas, Cassat and many other famed artists who loved the creativity the summers spawned. It became the talk of Paris and one would wonder all year if they too would become a part of this inner circle of renowned artists. I mention these holidays because it was within this world that Marlowe exposed himself to Nerissa and allowed her to become a necessity in his life. He taught her about art, nature and opened the world to her. What was left of the family was very close.

During Nerissa's sixteenth summer they fell in love and married. Much to Genevieve's dismay they would stay in Scotland. They remained there for a little over five years until the fateful night. Six months after his death in 1911 Nerissa had a son. She named him Marlowe Wemyss Lochalsh. That man was my Father. They, mother and son, like her parents and husband traveled to and from Scotland annually but only to visit and view her exhibits. The rest of the year was spent in Scotland being a mother and a painter. Nerissa never remarried. Her son Marlowe studied in Paris and became an interior decorator and married my mother Rochelle whom he met in school. Rochelle gave birth to a daughter Estelle Cara. That would be me. Scotland was not important to them like it had been to the rest of the family and although they did spend time there Marlowe felt the travel was too overwhelming each year. Because of this distance time went by where Nerissa would not see her family. He pleaded with his mother to relocate but his requests were unheard until she was too old to take care of herself. My father brought her to Paris where she spent the rest of her life in a nursing institution. In return Wemyss-Lochalsh never became a home to me until now.

When I was in University I spent a year abroad at Sarah Lawrence and loving New York never returned to Europe for any length of time. I spent my years then struggling with my lack of talent as a painter. I could paint but never became exceptional. We all have our own pains. In the end that path was not meant for me and having gotten a job as an assistant curator after graduation I began to develop my eye. Over time I became far more passionate about other artists as opposed to my straight-laced attempts. At twenty-seven I decided to open a gallery. With my fathers help and a loan from a bank we created Lochalsh in remembrance.

Have I done something great now when I look back at all the artists I have helped along the way or do I with each new talent that I discover feel the ache again? Augusta is a reminder of my own shortcomings and childhood dreams. Like a child can be to a mother. Yet for the first time I feel complete selflessness towards someone else's accomplishments. If I've learned anything from my years it is that the greatest disappointments can be the actual springboard into glorious opportunities. That is how it has been for me. I know it to be the same for my father who after my mother died in France returned to Scotland and lived his remaining days there. This brought him Peace. The love he manifested for life once again was not something he could have predicted.

Our first exhibit at Lochalsh was Mary Cassat. Her niece who had been like an Aunt to me remained a family friend over the years. She loaned me her personal collection which was made up of twenty-eight paintings for three months. It set the tone for my thematic home to women's art. For years we have been at the forefront of the women's artistic movement. I have exhibited ones that have come and gone without accolade, who had to endure what Nerissa did and seen the ones who were known as women receive ridicule and criticism. I have witnessed these heroic women through their work and have been lucky enough to show Georgia O'Keefe, Lee Kasner, Rosa Bonheur, Cecilia Beaux, Elizabeth A. Armstrong, Ellen Day Hale and many other powerful painters; I revere and cherish their courage.

Augusta as you know her now is a woman of twenty-five who has only just left childhood behind. Her work is of a woman's wisdom and studies the body and faces of the female sex. Sometimes her paintings remind me of the aged photographs taken by Julia Cameron. Her voice is strict and clear in her awareness of what lurks behind the eyes and needs to be expressed through the muscles of a hand. She shows the underworld of the body. She is unique ... she is an artistic genius. I feel I have found a daughter in her and our work together in these past months, almost a year now, have stirred other ideas and as we forge ahead in a number of different areas I find the excitement of collaboration in full force. In June of next year we will have an exhibit of male painter's for the first time and their portrayals of women. Somehow I had gotten too comfortable being a feminist. I am proud to be expanding my horizons due to the things I have learned from Augusta.

Finding my grandmother's journal has awakened and allowed me to examine my own judgments. And yet what I read is not nearly enough to know her. Was she wiser than the rest who so desperately try to move ahead to some unknown territory called happiness? For Nerissa remembrance and pain were not paralyzing. I have specifically learned from her that if we can be content within our circumstances we might then revel in the lives we are living and in that detachment find comfort even in death. We must remember that we do not lose a person when they die ... they hover nearby always, as if in another room of a large house. They are there steps away and although the door is closed and we can't see their faces if we listen long enough we will hear the steadiness of their breathing and the sound of their wings fluttering. My father is dead and though no single loss can compare I do not wish to erase the pain but to accept it as just another layer that I will live with. Nerissa strove through the fragments and in that striving alone discovered what living was.

    As I prepare an exhibit for my grandmother I feel the North Sea all around me and when I look back to where all this love of art began I know it to be from the first day she lifted a paintbrush there in Wemyss-Lochalsh. Maybe within those walls are more of her words and possibly next time, behind some book in the library I will chance upon her again.

The publication of this Diary is a toast to women all over the world and throughout time that have lost, longed for and found their voice, as she did. To artists ... they travel their soul each day and night and their art is the sum of their answers. To you, I raise my glass!

CPSIA information can be obtained
at www.ICGtesting.com
Printed in the USA
BVHW031635220622
640418BV00008B/271

9 781453 740064